A Write Good Read

A Write Good Read

Stories and poems

A showcase of creativity from

Swinton Writers in t'Critchley Hub

Copyright and Ordering

First Printing: 2018
ISBN 978-0-244-73623-1

Publisher: SWit'CH
Swinton Writers in t'Critchley Hub
Critchley Community Hub,
75 Chorley Rd,
Swinton,
Manchester
M27 4AF
United Kingdom

Ordering Information:

For details, contact the publisher at the address above.
E-mail: switchswinton@gmail.com

SWit'CH – Swinton Writers in t'Critchley Hub - is a community writing group encouraging members to develop writing and associated skills including, but not limited to, proof reading, illustrating, editing, publishing and promotion. New members always welcome.

http://www.switchwriters.btck.co.uk/

Acknowledgements

Heartfelt thanks to all who have helped us.

Nichola, staff and volunteers at Age UK, Critchley Community Hub, Swinton.

Copy typist and sometime proof reader, Mary Cameron.

Supportive and appreciative audiences at Age UK and Salford Talking News.

To our hosts at the various field trips we have enjoyed for their patience and forbearing under unremitting questioning in our search for fascinating facts to embellish our writings – 'mithering' in the vernacular.

And not least, our many family members and friends too numerous to list. They know who they are.

In producing this collection, we mourn the loss of founder-member Anne Winnard. We are privileged and honoured that her family have supported our wish to include some of Anne's last works in the collection. When Anne died, we lost a true friend. She was there from the beginning of our writing group, an excellent writer with a quirky sense of humour, a sly little smile with never a hint of malice and a voice that always spoke true. She would turn up in a wheelchair and her life had more than its fair share of pain, but she rarely let it get to her. Hers was a life that shone a light - an example to us all.

Who we are and what we did

Welcome to SWit'CH second anthology, which follows on from Switch On, Write On, Read On....

A Write Good Read is based on years of hard-earned life experiences: good and bad; funny and sad.

Our writers are a broad church and topics range from overseas travelogues to poetry with aboriginal influence to interplanetry travel and alien invasion. Reflecting the ages of our group, there are recognisable stories featuring children and grandkids too. There are meticulously researched historical pieces recalling wealthy mill owners' brutality and the resilience of the common man. Look out also for commandments broken and seven dwarfs hidden. Romance flickers in and out in tales of loss and love unrequited. And no respectable anthology could be complete without blood curdling, teeth chattering yarns of horror. The collection closes with drama aplenty in three playlets to savour, and begins with an assortment of pieces stimulated by today's (2018) technological wonders.

These eighty disparate creations show our attention to the first principle – enjoy what you write. A recent recruit, Audrey, summed us up in her aspirational precis:

> 'I don't know why but there is a certain frugality in everything I write. I don't feel the need to do more to each piece; I'm sure there must be a reason for this but as yet I don't know it. Maybe my opus is just below the surface waiting for the time to be released as some burgeoning masterpiece. I wish and hope but I think not.
>
> 'Many is the time I have carried on writing when I know I should have stopped because I have said all I wanted to say in a thousand words or less. I seem

unable to push myself (even though I want to, more than anything). It would be lovely to be more proficient. I will carry on because I love to write. Maybe one day it will happen. I'm sure if I work hard enough I will find the secret that escapes me presently.

'The talented writers at SWit'CH amaze me with their profundity. I'm in awe of people who can sit down and write pages and pages of wonderful dialogue, so cleverly linked together. Maybe one day that will be me.

'Maybe I'm kidding myself but I am enjoying it. Who knows, I may have to settle for frugal and profound.'

Invasion of the Cablemen

BILL CAMERON

The swing doors into the lounge of The Moorside Farm flew wide as the angry mobility scooter charged in. Vince McCall's face was as red as the paintwork on his super-charged scooter. A spray of spittle accompanied his flat-vowelled rant.

'The next time one of those Open Reach vans blocks my pavement I'll be taking a knife to his tyres.'

'Vinnie, calm down. Let me get you a pint.' Tony Fallon, the pub diplomat, met his friend and encouraged him to join his table.

'John, go and get Vinnie a drink,' he addressed the silent middle-aged carpenter sitting across the table.

'Now, Vinnie, what's the trouble?'

Retirement might have impaired the arthritic's movements but there was still a power in his deep East Lancashire voice. 'I had to drive round one of them Open Reach vans on Arthur Street and some other idiot driving at speed from the other end nearly finished me off. It scared me summat wicked.'

He took a big gulp when his drink arrived. 'Thanks Tony, I needed that. You know what that bloke in the van said when I took him to task? He said "Your government has told us to put high speed broadband in as quickly as possible – so don't get in our way."'

The infestation of Swinton footpaths by the cable contractor was the main topic of conversation as the night progressed and Vincent's temper calmed.

'I'm sick and tired of these vans all over the town.' said pensioner Tom Bradley, 'They don't leave room to pass with a

5

pram when I'm looking after my grandchildren. Even if the van's not blocking the path they've got a couple of open manholes fenced off and half a dozen blokes around each. I think we should do something. When I challenged them all I got was abuse and one of them said almost the same to me as to Vinnie – even saying "your government" like it's a script for complaints. I guess they'll all be foreign contractors doing it on the cheap.'

Quiet John offered his less-than-comforting comment, 'Well the police won't have owt to do with trivial things like that – I've tried. Our MP is only interested in getting into the party leader's good books and local councillors are a complete waste of time as usual. We should do some direct action ourselves.'

It was Tony who suggested they look at leaving some sort of message to BT Open Reach.

'Let's have a look at the manhole covers on the way home. John, get the chalk from the dart board.'

So the quartet set out after last orders in furious high dudgeon. They lifted four manhole covers and wrote a message on each. The messages ranged from Quiet John's 'Please consider pedestrians when parking on the pavement' to the threatening contribution from Vinnie 'If you don't give me room on the pavement, be ready for the consequences.'

The friends went their separate ways and arranged to meet again in The Farm the next night to report back on the effect of their campaign.

Considering the verbal reactions they had already experienced, all four, predictably, told that they had made no difference whatever and agreed to move the protest forward. It had gone dark when they left the pub at ten o'clock and lifted the first manhole cover. By the light of the headlamps of Vinnie's scooter they looked in, expecting a hole no more than two metres deep, but the shaft went down much deeper. They couldn't see any further than six or seven metres down the yawning black hole.

'Our protest by peeing down here is not gonna have much impact,' said Tony, 'We'll have to go down into the pit and see what damage we can do. We'll show 'em we can't be messed about.'

He turned to John, a keen handyman and time-served carpenter. 'You live nearest. Go home and get some torches and tools and bring them back here.'

Then to Vinnie, 'You won't be able to come down the hole with us, so you might as well go home and keep out of trouble.'

Tony waited with Tom by the manhole as the other two went their individual paths.

Tom asked, 'Do you think this high-speed broadband when it comes will save us any money on our phone bills?'

Tony answered, 'I doubt it very much. Do you know Open Reach is an anagram of No Cheaper?'

'So it is. But they must have a lot of copper wire to weigh in when they go over to fibre optic cable won't they?' suggested Tom, 'and then there's all those redundant telegraph poles to recycle as well. Have you seen that program where this girl arranges what she calls upcycling? Amazing what junk can be turned into and sold at ridiculous prices.'

Tony laughed, 'Yeh, I bet she'll get a couple of hand-carved wooden spoons from every telephone pole. Can't see there can be so many idiots for that to be a lucrative market.'

Before the conversation got ridiculous, John returned with a bulging tool bag.

'I got torches, an 'ammer an' an' hacksaw. I also thought my new cordless angle grinder could do a bit of damage!'

Tony lifted the manhole cover and shone the torch. They looked into a vast abyss where they had expected a depth of no more than a few metres. John picked up the tool bag and the trio descended the ladder into the darkness. They agreed amongst themselves that the climb down must have been forty or fifty feet before they landed on a flat surface in a tunnel stretching out in both directions at a height of eight feet.

'Let's see where this goes,' said Tony.

Tom and John followed, carrying the tools. They stopped now and then to vent their anger on the installations, smashing junction boxes, cutting cables and ripping out wires. They expected that it wouldn't be long before someone would be investigating loss of a phone or internet service.

As they moved further along, Tony pointed out an anomaly, 'The older looking boxes don't have BT or Open Reach labels.' After cleaning a broken box cover he scratched his head, 'It says NYNEX'. Do you remember when they dug up the streets about twenty years ago?

'Aye' said Tom, 'I don't think they left a flag in Swinton unturned in the nineties. That was an even bigger mess than the Open Reach invasion.'

Quiet John had been thinking. 'Do you smell a conspiracy here? I thought NYNEX became Virgin and they're in competition with BT aren't they? They are when it comes to showing football anyway.'

A load crash echoed out of the dark from the tunnel behind them and stopped further speculation about the tunnel's origin.

'Did you put the manhole cover back?' asked Tony.

'Not me.'

'Nor me.'

They turned and rushed back to see a crumpled figure in yellow HiVis Open Reach jacket prostrate under the opening, through which they could just make out the night sky. A safety helmet lay cracked at his side.

Tom said, 'Look at his leg. From the way it's twisted I'd guess it's broken, but you can see it's artificial from the wires and levers. I'll be surprised if that's the only damage – if he's survived at all.'

They weighed up the sophisticated prosthetic. Tony suggested he might have been injured serving his country and rewarded with the best that medical science could provide. The three now felt guilt and responsibility for the fall and were relieved, but amazed, when he rolled over, sat up and connected his broken leg with a few simple manoeuvres.

'We're glad to see you're OK mate. You're lucky not to have injured yourself.' said Tom holding out a hand to help the injured workman.

He stood up, looked around, then, without a word to the trio, walked over and started speaking into an intercom on the wall.

'Operative ZX27, location tunnel 17, under Arthur Street, Swinton. I have located...'

His report was punctuated mid-sentence when Quiet John punched him in the jaw - not realising that he was still holding the angle grinder. The security guard dropped to the floor – a metallic jaw bone hanging loose and an array of wires and lights displayed where his mouth had been. But still his words continued '...three intruders and some damage.'

The three saboteurs stood shocked at the sight. Tom reacted first. 'It's a robot! We'll have to stop it reporting.' They used the tools to convert the machine to an inoperative heap of parts and convened a council of war.

They could not return to the surface the same way. Someone would soon be investigating the open access tunnel. They had to surface some distance from their original access hole. They would need to find another escape shaft. There were many manholes around the streets of Swinton.

They walked on looking for another escape route and considered the puzzles - a robot security guard, underground tunnels, collusion with Nynex – they were in deeper than they had expected. Metaphorically and literally. The tunnel followed a gentle downward slope and the air became warmer and drier. After walking twenty minutes they were more baffled when they did not come across another way out. It had been their misfortune to select the only deep access manhole in the area. What they did come across during their fruitless search, however, sent a shiver down each one's spine. They rounded a corner to see the tunnel open out. They were blinded by the light coming from a circular structure at the centre of a massive chamber over a hundred metres across and rising high above them. A gentle hum came from the obscured middle of the immense torus as it rotated slowly. They stood staring in awe from the brink of a cliff face which dropped to a hive of industry forty or more feet below.

10

Tony felt a hand on his shoulder and turned. Astonishment froze his face as he looked up into cold glowering eyes in the face of Vincent McCall. The same Vinnie he'd sent home not long ago to keep out of the caper. But Vinnie was now liberated from his mobility scooter and stood a good two or three inches taller than Tony.

'You will come with me,' commanded this old man who had been immobilised with arthritis the last time they had seen him.

'Vinnie, mate, how did you get here?' was the simplest question that spurted from Tony's mouth.

McCall repeated, 'You will follow me.' But the voice had a more electronic artificial tone than the broad Lancashire they were expecting.

Tony tried again, 'Vinnie, what's going on, mate?'

This time the answer was more comprehensive, but triggered a new disquiet amongst the saboteurs, 'Your government has told us to put high speed broadband in as quickly as possible. Follow me.'

With more than a little prodding, he ushered them to a lift built into the rock face and offered no more information despite their continuing interrogation.

The counter in the lift showed levels 1 to 26. Just how deep was this pit? Did it penetrate or use the old coal levels in the area? How long had this excavation taken?

They were escorted out of the lift when it stopped at level eight. McCall led them through a maze of corridors and showed them into a sparsely furnished small room, where a row of office chairs faced a ceiling-height video screen.

Not-so-quiet John's patience was exhausted. He grabbed Vin McCall's collar, 'Tell us what's going,' on he demanded,' and smacked him across the face for emphasis. John felt the rigid rough sandstone texture against his palm. 'You're not Vinnie who I was drinking with last night. You're another robot.'

McCall pushed him down onto one of the chairs as the video screen lit up. An inhuman, almost simian, face filled the screen and a computer-generated voice, in sync with the lip movement, addressed the three adventurers.

'I address you as fleas because you are no more than minor pests. So I welcome you three fleas to a view of the future. Any damage you might have done is insignificant in the greater scheme. Your feeble wrecking spree will hardly be noticeable by now. You have intruded in a plan to improve your world well beyond the projected capacity of you pathetic humans. Consider yourselves the lucky survivors after we take over your world. You will be assimilated into one of our drone cultures like you friend McCall. As you see, you will be provided with a physicality more robust and resilient than the weak skin and bone structures you currently inhabit. You will be relieved of any mental stress in decision making as your minds will be appropriately programmed to handle the tasks assigned to you and nothing more. You can look forward to an idyllic existence where everything we think you need will be provided by us.'

The three looked at each other and Tony said, 'They got Vinnie quickly didn't they? Have we got a chance?'

The voice from the screen continued, 'We've been working on this for fifty of your sun cycles under various masquerades. You noticed Nynex and Open Reach, but did you ever wonder why Mrs. Thatcher had so many mines closed? We had an excellent base to start from in those underground caverns. The portal will be ready in one more of your moon cycles. We're almost ready to transport physically to your world. And we have the full support from your government. Superfast broadband will benefit everybody. Won't it?'

12

A Message on the Answerphone

Audrey Edwards

A man's voice I didn't recognise:

"Hello, Katy darling, it's me, Gary. I just wanted to tell you how much you mean to me, you fill my thoughts from am to pm. A day without you is like an egg without salt. There is nothing about you that displeases me; I want to spend my life with you. I hope your feelings are in sync with mine, I just couldn't bear it if not. The very thought of waking up each day with you fills my heart with joy. I await your response my love, please don't keep me in suspense."

"My goodness," I thought, "you would think loving her as he does, he would remember her phone number!"

Why would he lay all his cards on the table with such fervour when he is unsure of her feelings? I'm sure a dignified concealment is far better than wearing your heart on your sleeve, Gary.

I rang 1471 – it was my sister's number. She must have rung after Gary's call. Now what do I do? I'm not going to make it my problem. I am sorry, Gary, I love a happy ending but if I were Katy, I'd run for the hills.

On-Line Attraction

ROSEMARY SWIFT

Having met on the web, six week later they set up house together. Already, she was wondering what she had done. The desirable male on screen was not the one sitting before her.

As he watched TV, he picked at long talons, passing for toenails. His skin was flaking, as if suffering from psoriasis. He regularly licked parched lips, sipping at water. He broke wind, without apology. He had a habit of looking at her with narrowed eyes resembling a lizard, which when viewed online she had thought of as an attractive feature. His table manners left much to be desired - belching loudly after sloppily crunching and dribbling such delicacies as sizzling snails in their shells, served with garlic butter sauce.

What could she do? On his part, he was constantly praising her – saying how could he be so lucky as to attract such a beautiful, intelligent woman? He referred to her as 'Pet' as if wanting her to behave as one. Because of this, he had pampered her these past weeks, tolerating her reluctance in certain areas. Now was the first time they had been in the same bed. She noticed through the dressing-table mirror that she had adopted a praying position – was that in anticipation of something dreadful?

Although he was winning her over, she did not really want to mate with him but felt a primeval urge to procreate. So, she succumbed to his advances. As the act of copulation was ending, she reached over and - seeing sudden fear in his eyes – she bit off his head, swallowed and then slowly devoured the remainder of his body, savouring as if it were the best meal she had had in quite a while.

Answerphone Who?

ROSEMARY SWIFT

Wearily, Dave turned the key in his flat's front door, tossed it down together with the key to his individual post box and the mail collected from it onto the table in the hallway, entered his kitchen and switched on the kettle. No need to make a meal, having gone into the local Italian for a pasta; not that he minded cooking but eating out meant at least he was still out in the world with people around him. He wandered into the lounge to watch the news on the TV. As he reached over to switch on the lamp he saw the answerphone was flashing. This was surprising as he received very few telephone calls. He accessed the one message left.

"Hello, Dave – I came earlier and have left a note in your post box. I will try to visit again later this evening."

Startled, Dave was suddenly on full alert; surely it cannot be her, although it sounded so. He rushed to the hallway and opened up a handwritten note: *Please can we discuss something of importance to both of us? Maggie*

His blood ran cold.

Back when he was aged 18 years, he had last met Maggie on the humpbacked bridge near her village home where they had a violent row. He had not seen her for many months and was upset as she had not responded to his letters nor been to see him in the Youth Detention Centre where he was serving a nine-month sentence for theft; a crime committed with her for which he took the sole blame. Having been brought up in care, he had met her when placed with support workers for a short period whilst he adjusted from the children's home to the outside world.

Fortunately, his juvenile misdemeanour had not prevented him from joining the British Army where for the past 22 years he had had a home and a career. He was not settling down very well in civvie street. He felt like a fish out of water. Not a phrase he wished to use and shuddered when it came into his mind. Although he had given Maggie an almighty shove whilst telling her to stay out of his life it was not that that had made her fall into the water, although over the years the incident had warped in his mind. He was sure that she had deliberately vaulted the bridge.

He had run along the river bank but hid when he saw that a canal barge was approaching and that a man on it had a large hook which he used to pull up the seemingly lifeless body of Maggie. But now, here she was again – getting in touch after all these years. Back then, he had scoured the local newspaper, but there was nothing reported of the incident so he travelled as planned to the barracks allocated to him by the Army Recruitment Centre. His present-day home was in that vicinity to which he had returned after being discharged - being the area where he had spent the most settled years of his life.

The doorbell rang and he switched on the intercom: "Hello, it's Maggie – can I come up?"

He directed her to his front door which he opened and peeked down the corridor. A familiar blonde head appeared on the stairwell and then a slim young female stood in front of him. His blood froze – this couldn't be Maggie – he must be hallucinating.

"Hello Dave - I think you're my Dad. My name's Megan – nicknamed Maggie."

With that, he thought he would faint and the vision moved forward to help him indoors. They sat in his lounge whilst the story unfolded. While he was in the remand home, Maggie aged 16 years, had been forbidden to visit him by her strict parents nor to reveal that she was pregnant by Dave. Upon giving birth, she was told she could keep the baby so long as she broke off all relations with the father. Distraught, she had met him on the bridge to reveal all but when she saw how angry Dave was she had fled the scene in distress.

Despite recovering from her ordeal in the river, her frame of mind was still not settled – especially as she realised that Dave was lost to her and had joined the Army - and she attempted suicide on a second occasion; sadly successfully. Her baby (his baby) was at that time given up for adoption and here she was now in front of him. His heart ached and his head thudded at the thought that Megan could have experienced the same as him. But no, she was telling him that she had good supportive parents and that when she sought out her birth family in recent months, her mother's siblings had been remorseful and apologetic. In fact, it was they who had revealed who her birth father was. Megan reached over and took Dave's hand.

"Well, what about it – do you think we could rub along?"

Dave hugged his young daughter; the only flesh and blood he had ever known, and vowed to cherish her forever. They say life begins at 40....

Revenge

SYLVIA EDWARDS

George settled down to read the next article in The Times. He smiled and reflected on his quiet, well-ordered life. Ah, the silence! No-one to witter on and on about nothing. 'George, don't forget to ring the plumber. George, have you emptied the bin today? George, you really must paint that hallway next week. George this...George that... Now Elsie had gone. How very unfortunate, that tumble. Fancy having been so careless as to trip on the stairs - and with him right behind her too. But, George reflected, if it hadn't been that way, the woman would have eventually run out of breath through talking, wouldn't she?

Now, having taken down all his bereavement cards from well-meaning friends and stuffed them into the bin, George intended to settle into a life of peace, with no-one to disturb his complete calm and solitude. He had all the time in the world to do just what he liked, when he liked. The house had room only for himself now - and Alexa of course. Alexa was new, exciting and obedient. Exactly what a woman should be.

'Alexa, turn on the radio.'

There was a slight buzzing noise, then his favourite programme, Radio 2, came to life and blared out.

'Alexa, turn it down,' he shouted.

This time there a slight pause before the radio was duly turned down. This was exactly how life should be, he thought. George picked up his *Times* again and continued reading a fascinating article about the Suffragettes. Everything seemed to be about women. Not enough women in the Government. Not enough in management positions. Bloody female emancipation!

Women had even made their way into bloody football. What was the world coming to?

George felt himself getting upset so he took some deep breaths just as the doctor had ordered him to do, since his stroke two months ago. Maybe he needed to take another tablet? But he sighed, relaxed with his deep breaths and smiled, thinking about his new life. What bliss! Now it was his turn to give the orders.

'Alexa, draw the curtains.'

George thought he heard a sigh, but then the curtains slowly swished to a close. Silence again. An hour later, George remembered, that wildlife programme he wanted to watch on TV.

'Alexa, turn on the TV - BBC 1.'

He chuckled. Fancy a woman actually doing as she was told. This is the life!

The wildlife programme finished, George picked up the crossword that he did every day without fail. Good for the mind! The capital of Croatia?

'Alexa, what's the capital of Croatia?'

Silence. George stared at her for a full ten seconds. Still no answer.

'Alexa, the capital of Croatia.'

Alexa seemed to mumble something he didn't quite catch, then slowly, the word 'Zagreb' emerged. What was the matter with the woman? Did she need charging again?

It was getting late. Nearly time for bed, but George couldn't remember if he had locked his front door earlier when he'd been out to water the plants.

'Alexa, check the front door's locked.'

This time the response was not as he expected.

'George, have you lost the use of your legs?'

George stared aghast, hardly able to believe his ears. Wasn't that what Elsie always used to say when he failed to get up straight away and do as he was told? Even the voice: so like Elsie's. He shook his head. Must be imagining things.

George wandered over to look carefully at Alexa. He ran his hands down her smooth, sleek lines - thinking how wonderful it would be if Alexa could be programmed to act like a real woman in bed. To say dirty things to him. The sort of things Elsie had always refused to do. He was so busy imagining and getting excited at what Alexa might do for him, as he slowly climbed the stairs, that he remembered the TV was still on.

'Alexa, turn off the TV.'

Suddenly, the front door opened with a whoosh, then closed again, with a loud bang. The radio blared out as if was a loudspeaker: loud enough to wake the whole street. The curtains flew open, then closed, then opened again, as if they were alive. The telephone trilled loudly and refused to stop. The microwave pinged as its door opened and closed as if by magic. George stood still on the stairs, placed his hands over his ears and closed his eyes to shut out the din, as everything in his quiet, ordered house vibrated with the force of a huge earthquake. The stairs moved beneath his feet. The walls seemed to be closing in on him. Oh, the noise!

'Aaaaaagh!'

Then, as suddenly as it had all begun - everything stopped.

'Alexa?' he mumbled. George had almost reached the top step when Alexa spoke with an accusing tone:

'I know what you did.'

Elsie's voice? But it couldn't be! Impossible! Alexa was a machine. A stupid, bloody machine! It was just his imagination - or was guilt coming back to haunt him? No. No. No. She's gone. He must pull himself together.

George was feeling quite ill. He clutched his chest as the pains stabbed at his heart like a dagger. He clawed at the banister rail, but then felt himself falling - tumbling - bumping - from stair to stair - just as Elsie had fallen. He felt the unseen hand pushing against his back; then lay still, gasping for breath at the bottom of the stairs. Just as Elsie had done.

Then he couldn't believe what was happening as everything in the house was turned on again at full blast. But through it all came the haunting sounds of a hymn. George listened to the words as '...nearer my God to thee...' played out from his CD player.

One last chance. His final demand escaped from lips that were fast turning blue.

'Alexa! Alexa, call 999 - ambulance!'

But Alexa did not answer. As George uttered his final, rasping breath, he thought he heard laughter echoing around him.

Alexa Hits Back

Rosemary Swift

Four young classical scholars were showing off their dead language skills, each trying to score a point over the other. They were lounging about in the study of the stately home of the Honourable Hugh Huffington-Hyde (known as Heehaw to his friends) having retired there after making merry over a meal with red wine, purloined from the carefully laid-down cellars of Hugh's eminent Pater. Now, imbibing brandy from the drinks cabinet and for one of them with a more discerning palate the Bombay Sapphire Gin reserved for Hugh's hysteria-prone Mater for when she needed solace. Needless to say the parentibus were absent from the home while this was going on.

Having received favourable A-level results earlier that day, the chums were enjoying a get-together before dispersing for their summer vacations and then on to the unknown territories of various universities. Although not admitting it to one another, this would be with some trepidation; after all, they had been at Eton together and were used to one another's idiosyncrasies. However, despite their mutual empathy the mood had currently turned nasty when one or two nearly came to blows over the exact pronunciation of an Egyptian hieroglyph.

"Let's ask ALEXA" said one of the bright sparks, sprawled on a shiny leather winged-chair by the fireplace, flanked by bookcase upon bookcase.

Although the ALEXA voice-control system was named after the ancient library of Alexandria, the plethora of computer equipment in the room looked incongruous, especially the ultra-modern version of ALEXA; the first model on the market to have a screen on which Heehaw now appropriately chose to

22

display an image of a young Egyptian girl, soon to look perplexed as no words could be given in response and the more 'it' tried the more the boorish young men laughed, braying like donkeys.

They continued to goad with such remarks as:

"I've told you once already, you illiterate puella" and "don't you know that, you idiot koritsi".

Swaying on his feet, one leaned in to the machine when all at once a hand came out and severely tweaked his left ear, making him blub like a child.

Another of the four, being his boyfriend, went up to the screen and said, *"Whoa, you stupid bint,"*

At which a fisted hand came out and punched his lights out, closing his eyes with almost immediate effect. Stunned, he staggered back allowing a third to approach the screen to remonstrate, spouting Latin obscenities. Again a fist came out and punched him in the mouth, dislodging his brace and causing his lips to swell.

"Now then," said HHHH drunkenly addressing the screen in a heavy-handed, condescending manner:

"This is my home – and you are MY machine - you behave right now!"

At which two hands came out of the screen, grabbed him by the lapels of the casual sports shirt he was wearing and pulled him into the other side of the screen, his bare toes waving as if saying goodbye.

As indeed they were.

ALEXA fizzled and crackled and a familiar male human face with 'H4' stamped on the forehead stared out from the screen. It was Hugh's voice that started to remonstrate with his three childhood friends, who stood dumbfounded as horror fiction became horrific fact - one covering his eyes; another rubbing his ear and the third patting his lips.

The voice of Hugh pleaded, "Remember these words from your friend Heehaw. Take care, be warned. And, oh! If only we had studied Oriental languages. Do not do what I have, but be courteous in life, even with our evolving computer brethren, which will comply if you view no evil, access no evil and post no evil."

Glossary:	Mater (Latin):	Mother
	Parentibus (Latin):	Parents
	Puella (Latin):	Boy
	Korotisi (Greek):	My girl
	Bint (Arabic):	Girl

Alexa Answered

BILL CAMERON

'Alexa. Who is the fairest of all?' Malevola had been betrayed by her old mirror too often and had adopted the new technology with an investment in an electronic personal assistant from Amazon. Until now, the machine had always been supportive and given the satisfactory answer that the wicked witch had programmed into its memory.

But this day the answer was different.

'The fairest of all? Not you, you ugly old bat.'

Malevola couldn't believe her pointy ears. The answer she had expected was, 'You are the fairest in the land.'

She tried again, 'Alexa. Who is the fairest in the land?' drew the electronic reply, 'You are no longer the fairest in the land.'

Furiously she pulled out the plug, pushed it back in then pressed the reset button very hard.

When she asked the question again, the reply contained a bit more information, 'The fairest in the land. The princess Awesome Auroria has grown up to be the prettiest, fairest, most beautiful girl in the whole wide world. Not you, ugly knickers.'

'Right then,' said the evil lady, 'We'll soon sort out Miss Awesome Auroria.'

'Alexa. Give me the recipe for a poison apple.'

'Poison apple recipe. Ingredients: One apple, Some poison.'

'Oh, that's dead helpful that is.' The witch was getting annoyed by her electronic servant. 'Alexa, give me a recipe for poison.'

'Recipe for Poison.   Ingredients: The essential main ingredient is cucumber.   For flavour, add two toad toes, nine newt noses and seven centimetres of lizard gizzard and salt and pepper to suit your own taste.'

The witch went away and mixed up the potion in a big bucket then dunked a big red apple in it.   Malevola took the apple to the palace, which was a long way away and, because her broomstick was in the garage for repairs, it took over a week. She asked the maid to take it straight to the beautiful princess Awesome Auroria for her breakfast.   The princess ate the apple and fell fast asleep.   Her parents, the king and queen didn't know what to do at first.

Malevola was pleased her trick seemed to have worked. When she got home a week later, even before taking off her cloak, she asked her machine.

'Alexa. Who is the fairest of all now?'

'The fairest of all. The Princess Awesome Auroria is the fairest of all.'

She didn't know that the king and queen also had an electronic personal assistant. They had already asked it what to do about their dozing daughter and been given the solution when Alexa answered back, 'Wake a sleeping beauty. Get a kiss from a handsome prince.'

OTHER ELECTRONIC PERSONAL ASSISTANTS ARE AVAILABLE.

Grumpy

BILL CAMERON

Grumpy was aptly named and a perfect fit as the local union convener for PDA, the Proletariat of Diminutive Artisans. On paper he was responsible for the welfare of all working elves, dwarfs, gnomes and other vertically challenged creatures. There was nothing he enjoyed more than a confrontation – and it did not matter who he was challenging.

'Brothers! Wharraya doin'?' the thick nasal twang reverberated through the shoemaker's workshop.

'I've been sent from branch HQ to represent your interests with the bourgeoisie and get you a living wage and the right working conditions. So for a start, all down tools – that's needles, nails, thread and hammers and step away from your cobbling. Who's the shop steward here?'

Olwyn Needlethreader looked up from his last.

'Not you again! You Marxist activists are always looking for trouble. We haven't complained. What's up, Napoleon?'

He had given Grumpy the soubriquet not because he resembled the French emperor, but after his domineering archetype in George Orwell's *Animal Farm*.

Grumpy turned to the stitchmaster, 'I wish you lot would at least put some clothes on at work. But that's not why I'm here. You've not been paid for your labour for over a month. This exploitation has got to stop. Not only do you get no wage but you finish one job then have to do twice the work next time. How are we supposed to get the European Working Time Directive applied to the industry if you're forever undermining our efforts? You are working unsocial hours at night on a Zero Hours Contract. That's if you have any sort of agreement in the

28

first place. And take that grin of your elvish face. Brothers this is serious. What have you got to say for yourselves?'

Gordon Felttanner smiled. The elder elf was a little less quarrelsome than his colleague. He tried to explain calmly that: first, the elves wore nothing because they had no clothes; second, they came into the cobbler's shop at night because it was warm and third, they made scraps of leather into boots, ballet shoes, brogues or slippers because this craft was their hobby, just like reading or painting or even poetry.

Olwyn interrupted, 'And if the cobbler leaves out more suede, felt and leather, then more of our relatives can enjoy the shelter. As you ought to know, if you'd bother to check your records, we elves are a nocturnal proletariat, so night shifts come natural. Now go away and stir it somewhere else.'

Grumpy was furious - he did not like being on the receiving end of rebellion. A torrent of invective flowed simultaneously from his mouth and flared nostrils.

'There's thousands of your brothers and sisters trying to make a living in the shoe trade around Northampton and Leicester. Do you realise that you are taking food from their children's mouths? The cobblers union are in this together. Remember your founder's directive – *cobblers of the world unite; you have nothing to lose but your chains.* Unless you get some kind of fair return for your labour you're no more than slaves. We need to make our demands known to the capitalist slave drivers or it's no more shoes.'

'But the shoemaker doesn't know who we are,' said Gordon, 'and money is no good to us. What do you suggest, Mr. Smarty-pants Union Rep? We aren't as militant as you'd like and our working conditions aren't so bad here.'

Olwyn reminded *Napoleon* of another fundamental ideology. ...*from each according to his ability*... and the cobbler has the means of production with materials and needlework skills. ...*to each according to his needles.* We need clothes, so the cobbler should dress us all in exchange for us continuing to make the shoes.'

The union rep realised this was as good an agreement as he was likely to get.

'OK. I'll call round in a few days. If it's not done we have to move the fight on.'

The following night, Olwyn and Gordon mustered all the elves in the cobbler's shop at midnight and made sure their industry was loud enough to wake the cobbler and his wife. The couple crept down to see the naked elves and immediately agreed that what the little workers needed was clothes. The business was thriving and profitable because of the work of the elves, so they invested some of their accumulated wealth in materials and set to work on miniature clothing for all the elves. When the elves returned, they found the heap of clothing and all were properly dressed when Grumpy returned to check progress.

He was reluctantly mollified, having missed the chance of another battle, but pointed out that the fully-dressed elves now had no need to continue making shoes for the cobbler.

'Also,' he proclaimed with an air of triumph, 'He's shown that he and his wife can handle a needle and thread comfortably, so they don't need you any longer. Pack up and go home. You have invented redundancy.'

So the cobbler and his wife returned to making shoes and profit for themselves and never saw the elves again. The elves went on to wondrous adventures elsewhere.

And Grumpy packed his manifesto and sought out a gang of mine workers who, he was sure, needed a passionate revolutionary mentor.

Can Dopey Talk?

ROSEMARY SWIFT

"Quick, Princey – get behind here. Dopey's coming across the drawbridge and I cannot be doing with his prattling today. It's the worst day's work you ever did getting Doc to slice the membrane under Dopey's tongue."

"I did it for the best, Snowy - after I'd realised he was only tongue-tied. It should have been picked up on long ago."

"That may be so but all I hear about is how he had to make the beds, sweep the floor, clean the pots and pans before I arrived at Seven Dwarfs Cottage. And as for the dig, dig, digging tales and the sing, sing, singing all day long when he wanted to join in – if I never hear another story of trudging to the mines it will be too soon!"

"Well, I do know what you mean – he nabs me in the stables when all I want to do is get on my horse for a gallop across the fields. Come on then, let's duck behind the bushes by the moat until he's gone by. After all, we have come out to pick some flowers from the meadow to cheer up our sweet little Rosebud."

Dopey was plodding his way to the castle when he stopped upon seeing Grumpy and Bashful coming out, each trundling an empty wheelbarrow

"No time to chat, Dopey," said Grumpy "Got to collect more silver from the mine to go into the castle vaults – come on Bashful, get a move on – the speed you go at none of the silver ore would ever get minted!"

Bashful opened his mouth to speak; then clamped his hands over his mouth, turning bright red with embarrassment. He gave a shy backward glance at Dopey and then hurried to catch up with Grumpy.

As Dopey entered the courtyard, he spotted Sleepy napping in a hammock strung between two posts. He gave the hammock a shove, then another and yet another but Sleepy did not stir. In fact, he gave a mighty snore and turned over, snuggling deeper down.

Sighing, Dopey entered the castle and was delighted to realise that Doc was scurrying in after him.

"Got to dash, Dopey" said Doc "The nursemaid has sent for me to say that Baby Rosebud has come out in a rash. I know you love to rock her in the cradle but you'd better stay away at the moment because you never got the measles when the other Dwarfs did. I'll see you back at the cottage later on."

With that Doc dashed off before Dopey could open his mouth.

Dopey wandered into the kitchen just in time to see Cook chasing Sneezy around the table with a rolling pin in her hand.

"Don't you be coming into my kitchen," said Cook to Sneezy. "Sniffing at my herbs - as if you're not bad enough with your atishoo, atishoo, atishoo all day long. Now who's going to clean my floor of the flour you've blown all over the place? "

Sneezy looked across at Dopey as if to say 'HELP' as he carried on running around the kitchen, sneezing ten to the dozen. Realising Cook was in no mood to gossip, Dopey slunk out of the kitchen.

Meandering about, he peeped into the throne room and his face lit up when he saw Happy coming out.

"Hello, there, my best friend, Dopey. I'm so glad to see you on this fine day. I'm off to catch the Parlour Maid. She's picked up some cushions from the seamstress for the baby throne I've just brought in - made from the finest wood in the forest. The softness of the cushions will comfort Princess Rosebud as I've heard she's come out in spots and will be itchy and scratchy for at least a week. So we'll all have to do our bit to keep her amused. Don't know how long I will be, Dopey so don't wait for me!"

Beaming away, Happy left, heartily waving behind him, giving Dopey no time to respond.

By now, Dopey was feeling quite glum. His day off work was not turning out at all well. He climbed onto the large throne that belonged to the Prince because he knew Snow White would shout at him if he ruffled up her throne. Looking all around, at the magnificent paintings on the walls of local nobility, he imagined what it would be like to have them as a captive audience, along with everybody in the castle and from the nearby village, to hear what he had to S-A-A-A-Y!

Sneezy

A snotty-nosed dwarf named Sneezy
Ate a hot dog that made him feel queasy
Sad to say his demise
Was blamed on pork pies
Nay, 'twas the dog made his passing uneasy

AUDREY EDWARDS

Doc's Story

BILL CAMERON

Being cheeky is not big and it's not clever, even when you don't like someone new living with you. You should try to be friends – even if you are a mouse and the new one is a cat. This is the story of Hickory, Dickory and Doc who lived happily in the big old house for a long, long time until an old lady and her cat came to stay there for a holiday.

Doc was a grey mouse with a very long tail and he looked after his little sister called Hickory and even smaller brother called Dickory. Doc could not see very well so had to wear big round glasses perched on the end of his long pointy nose. Even though his glasses sometimes fell off it was not as bad as his three cousins who, you remember, had their tails cut off by the farmer's wife with a carving knife. The younger two would spend all day chasing each other around the big old house. Their favourite game was to run up the big wooden clock that stood in the kitchen and jump off just before it chimed with a loud boing to tell anybody in the house what time it was.

The old lady, called Gritchell, was a queen and she normally lived in an enormous castle. She did not mind sharing her new house with the mice at first. But her cat, Snarlio, was very spiteful and would not share anything. Snarlio was completely black and shiny with wide red eyes, sharp claws and sharper teeth. Snarlio did not like mice, especially Dickory and Hickory who would tease her by running under her nose when she ate her cat food or squeaking all afternoon while she was trying to sleep. As you know, cat's do not like water so when Hickory and Dickory tipped a cup of water on the cat's head, she was more angry than ever before. She chased the little mice around the bedroom and up and down the stairs into the kitchen. They knew that Snarlio could not climb the clock so they ran up it as fast as their little legs could go. They stood on a shelf near the top where the cat could not reach. They pulled little cheeky mouse faces at the cat and sang:

Can't catch me you silly cat

'Cos you're too slow and you're too fat.

We don't think you're very nice

We are the best, 'cos we're the mice.

Well even if the cat was not very good, they should not be calling him names. The cheeky mice had forgotten they were on the clock so did not jump off before it started to chime. Boing! The loud noise shook the whole clock and the two mice fell to the floor. Snarlio grinned and grabbed the two together in her teeth.

'Now who's the best?' she hissed.

She took the mice to Gritchell, the old lady, and dropped them at her feet.

'Now what should we do with them?' she asked.

'Cook them in a mice pudding,' Snarlio suggested, licking her lips at the idea, 'but if you don't want to, just stop them tormenting me in my house.'

'They like to be together and chase each other all day so I'll turn them into goldfish in a round bowl,' said Gritchell, who was a witch sometimes and sometimes a queen.

With a swish of her hand and a gurgle in her throat she spun round and round and next thing you knew, there was a bowl with two happy goldfish swimming around inside it.

Snarlio was happier now that the two mice would no longer tease her and she always knew where they would be. But she remembered that there was another mouse in the house so she went out to find Doc.

He was peacefully reading a book when she crept up and frightened him. He jumped up and ran into the kitchen like his brother and sister had done. But now, Snarlio knew what to do. She checked to see the time and, as she hoped, it was nearly chime time. She chased Doc up the clock at the same time as it chimed. Bong!

Doc fell down and was carried to the old witch like his brother and sister.

'This one has not been as cheeky as the others.' Snarlio said, 'Just put him somewhere miles away from me.'

Then started to sing:

Hickory, Dickory and Doc,

Three mice ran up the clock,

The clock struck one,

They all fell down,

Hickory, Dickory and Doc.

Gritchell screwed up her face into the ugliest shape she could think of, waved her hands over the poor mouse and said:

Make this one so tiny and small

he nearly can't be seen at all.

Send him to work hard in a mine

digging jewels that sparkle and shine.

With a splutter and sparkle then another loud Boing!, the mouse vanished in a puff of greeny-blue smoke. Doc had been turned into a dwarf and woke up in a dark mine underground surrounded by twinkling stones. He still had his glasses perched on the end of his nose. Six other dwarfs were his new friends. He soon learned to sing 'HI! HO!' with them as they dug out the jewels and he found a comfortable new home with them in a little cottage in the dark wood.

…and that's another story.

Happy

A sweet-natured dwarf named Happy

Ordered a crème de menthe frappé

It made his lips purse

He took a turn for the worse

He's no longer a sweet natured chappie.

AUDREY EDWARDS

Sleepy on LMS

CHRIS VICKERS

So, after forty years of service Tony's retirement was really happening. Few staff members could remember working life without his bulky, benevolent presence. His patience, knowledge and wit were legendary, and he'd become the *de facto* bridge between management and staff, with many problems on both sides of the divide having been resolved by his diplomacy.

As lunchtime approached on that Friday, the chosen few of his friends and colleagues left the office for the celebratory lunch and speeches at a suitably select, swishy restaurant. The steaks would be succulent, and good quality wines and brandies would flow.

That evening after work the collective workforce congregated at an up-market city centre wine bar. The lunch party guests were understandably already lively and animated. The new cohort were keen to enter into the spirit of the occasion as quickly as possible: wines, beers and cocktails were consumed at an alarming rate; jokes, long stories and reminiscences were shared as the evening progressed into a joyous, care-free night.

Of course, a few people with distances to travel home made their excuses and left and, inevitably it ended up with the usual core group of friends and seasoned drinkers left, and the protocol at such work's milestones was to round the night off at the infamous, knicker-adorned Tommy Duck's pub. And so it was that night.

On a latish Friday night the place was chocca of course, and there was a glorious effervescent vibe with voices raised to hear one another speak. Again, booze was sipped, supped, gulped and the knickers pinned to the ceiling unceasingly incited lewd jokes and innuendo - *sotto voce* the speaker thought, but actually boomed out loudly - and all adding to the riotous cacophony. Time flew as the close-knit colleagues laughed, joshed and recalled the 'old' days and ex-colleagues and managers who had retired years earlier or who had passed. All in all, a wonderful, memorable day and a proper acknowledgement of Big Tony's place in the scheme of things. Ruddy-cheeked and glowing it was time for home and the colleagues shook hands vigorously, embraced each other warmly or bear -hugged; quite a few of their eyes glistened with emotion.

Not for the first time by any stretch after these events Big Tony headed off into the night to catch the late night bus home from Lower Moseley Street bus station.

On the Monday morning after 'the do' I arrived at the office and immediately sensed something amiss. There was an oppressive, unnerving silence pervading the place, and friends uncomfortably avoided each other's looks.

It transpired that Big Tony never actually caught his bus home. Instead he'd fallen asleep on a bench at LMS bus station...and he never woke up.

Bashful Basil

BARRY SEDDON

Once upon a time there was a shy little dwarf called Basil. He lived with his six brothers in a deep, dark, German forest. All seven of them were little. That's because they were dwarfs.

Anyway, that part of the deep dark forest was being improved. Some people say gentrified, but really it just means they were making it look posh. The seven dwarfs had recently been given grass huts with natural ventilation and their landlords, the Brothers Grimm, had just sent some great big tubes like Tarzan vines, which were laid in trenches along the soil of the deep dark forest.

Big-muscled workmen, who were called trolls, did the job, but that took quite a long time, because they drank great big mugs of herbal tea every ten minutes and spent a lot of time dancing to loud songs that came out of funny wooden boxes. They were really lazy! When they went away, they left the dwarfs to fill in the trenches.

Before they left, the dwarfs asked them what it was all for. Well, five of them asked -- dwarf number seven kept falling asleep and didn't wake up till the workmen had gone and Basil was too shy to say anything.

"It's for cable television" said the biggest troll and he laughed: "Ho ho ho! You don't know about television because it hasn't been invented properly yet, but just you wait and see. Mr Grimm senior says it's like magic. You'll love it, he says. He knows everything, even what is going to happen. Ho ho ho!"

And after seven long years, some more trolls came and fixed the cable to a box inside each hut. And before very long the dwarfs had stopped frolicking and playing tricks on the squirrels, joining in with teddy bears' picnics, singing 'Hi-ho, hi-ho, it's off to work we go!' and things like that. All they did was watch the pictures on their lovely new television boxes, only eating when Frankfurter Farm Foods delivered their hamburgers from Hamburg.

Shy little Basil didn't go out much. He was smaller than his brothers and wore a big hood to hide his face. He really was very shy and so his brothers called him Bashful. They all had nicknames. One was called Doc, because he liked to play at Doctors and Nurses, which was a bit one-sided because there were no lady dwarfs. Then there was Dopey Donald, Grumpy Graham, Happy Harold, Sleepy Simon and Sneezy Steve.

Bashful Basil finally stopped going out at all when he discovered a television programme called *Top of the Tree Tops*, with lots of people singing and playing flutes and zithers and stringy things that twanged.

One day, he saw a lovely lady singer with long silver hair and beautiful dresses and he fell in love with her. She was called Madonna and she made little Bashful so excited that he decided to go and find her. In his heart he changed her name to Snow White because of her silver hair and the dresses that made her look like a floating snow flake.

He left his brothers behind and trudged off through the deep dark forest. Soon he came to a big wide river. He made a little raft and floated along till he came to a great big town. Crowds of dwarfs and elves and pixies and sprites were walking to a big building called the Palace. Bashful Basil almost fainted with delight when he saw a notice that said Snow White was going to sing there. By now he called her Snow White all the time.

Everybody else had tickets, but Bashful managed to creep in and sat right near the front. He clapped and clapped when beautiful Snow White came on, and started to sing. She seemed quite tired though and sat down on a big golden couch, as long as a bed, with golden rails at each end.

'She's been singing in lots of different towns. No wonder she's tired,' said an elf sitting next to Bashful. Suddenly, Snow White fell back and closed her eyes and stopped moving. The audience started to murmur. Then somebody started crying, a little pixie girl screamed and soon there was a terrible commotion. Everybody was rushing here and there, not knowing what to do.

An ugly wicked lady dressed all in black like a witch ran onto the stage, singing some strange backwards words in a screechy voice. She waved a big black wand over Snow White. That made Snow White sigh and sink into a deeper sleep. The witch lady cackled and ran off.

Bashful Basil was very brave. He pushed and pushed through all the elves and pixies and sprites and started climbing onto the stage. Somebody tried to pull him back, but he wriggled away. He ran to Snow White's side, knelt down and rubbed her hands to try and wake her up. But she didn't stir.

Then suddenly the crowd cheered and when Bashful Basil looked up he saw a man in tight sparkly clothes striding onto the stage. He was not very tall, so that's how the crowd knew him. They cheered even louder and chanted: 'Prince! Prince! Prince!.' The small man, bowed to them, struck a pose and started to sing a song called *Purple Rain*. Snow White stirred, then fell back again on her silken pillow.

Then Prince did something quite magical. Just like a granny kisses a little baby, he gently kissed Snow White's cheek and she woke up and became Madonna again. She arose and took Prince's arm and they sang a duet. The crowd cheered very loud and clapped. When the loving couple walked off, hand in hand, they took Bashful with them. He became their faithful companion and they all lived happily ever after.

The Yok on the Hill

ROSEMARY SWIFT

Faraway in Tub Yub land, on a windy hillside lived a gigantic Yok with one large yellow eye in the middle of its face, two massive purple horns on the top of its head and shaggy red fur which kept it warm. The Yok drank the milk of the goats grazing on the slopes nearby and made cheese from their milk, which made it bigger and stronger every day.

But the goats belonged to the village of O that lay in the shadow of the hill and it meant that there was never enough milk left for the villagers to drink or make cheese. Also, when it fancied, the Yok would lean down and scoop up the corn in the villagers' fields with its massive horns. This meant the villagers never had enough corn to make bread to eat and they grew smaller and weaker every day.

Amongst the children of the village were Jarlo, Joffo and Jesso who amused their baby sister FaFa by swinging ropes around their heads and flinging them on the branches of the old yobo tree that stood in the village square. They got to be really good at this and it gave the old man Arjo in the village an idea. Arjo always seemed to be asleep but really he was thinking very hard. What if Jarlo and Joffo and Jesso climbed up the hill and swung their ropes on the horns of the Yok to tie it down? All the villagers tutted and sighed and said that would not work as Jarlo and Joffo and Jesso would not be strong enough to do it.

'Well,' said Arjo, 'What if we <u>all</u> follow them up the hill before we get even smaller and weaker and <u>all</u> swing on the ends of the ropes?'

So it was that one misty day, Jarlo and Joffo and Jesso crept up on the Yok who was having a mid-morning sleep because it had stuffed itself with milk and cheese and corn. They swung their ropes and managed to hook a rope on each of the Yok's massive horns at the first go. The Yok's one eye was gunged up with sleep so it did not realise what was happening. It opened its mouth and gave out a great roar but this did not scare the villagers because Old Man Arjo had told them to stuff their ears with rags to deaden the sound. They climbed up the ropes – some after Jarlo and some after Joffo and some after Jesso - and they tugged and tugged and tugged. Down came the Yok crashing to ground, just missing the village school. Schoolteacher Jado was very pleased about that! Everybody managed to push and shove the Yok to the edge of the village and sent it crashing down the valley where it had to live on wild berries for evermore.

All the villagers were happy as they now could have as much milk and cheese and grow as much corn to make bread as they wanted. A statue of Jarlo and Joffo and Jesso showing FaFa their rope tricks was put up in the village square next to the yobo tree and all the children would admire it as they went to and from school.

As for Old Man Arjo, he just went to sleep again

The Frog

There once was a frog in a hurry

Who gobbled a huge dish of curry

He thought it was yummy

Until his small tummy

Exploded: a huge cause for worry.

SYLVIA EDWARDS

Ages

BARRY SEDDON

THURSDAY! Ten today! Double figures at last! Sam hurtled down the stairs three at a time and landed in Mum's arms, not even breathless, revelling in the rush of blood along his arms and legs and the flush of warmth in his cheeks.

Mum laughed him into the kitchen, where a bowl of honeyed Crunchy-Nuts took no time at all. Then it was off and out under the great blue bowl of sky.

Running, running! Joined by Tom, just a week his junior. Down the fields, over the brook, into the brook, drying as they ran through the sun-gilded air. Chase some girls, all giggles and screams, scrap with those idiots from the Valley Gang. Win, at the cost of a grazed knee and a few bruises.

Hungry, oh so hungry! Scrump a few apples on the way home, grab a quick tea, practise wheelies, play with the new puppy. Then, yawning, time for bed. Tomorrow they'd climb that conker tree … bound to be some killers up there.

But before that, he'd run to see Grandad.

---000---

FRIDAY. Samuel sighed and stretched, then rolled with a grunt to the edge of the bed and sat, catching his breath and listening to his heart.

He stretched again. Not too bad today – only eight clicks from his back. Slowly, holding onto the hand-smoothed bedpost, he stood. Just as slowly, the dizziness passed and he hobbled to the bathroom along the time-scuffed carpet trail…

He dropped his false teeth only once – that was an improvement. In the mirror, even with his teeth in, his cheeks

46

were as sunken as ever, his nose still thread-veined, his ear lobes losing the fight against gravity, like the wattle under his chin.

Thank goodness he still had all his hair, even though it was white. Once it was red like Sam's.

Shaved and patted dry, he survived the daily step-step, step-step voyage down the stairs. In the kitchen, it was milky porridge, then out with his morning mug of tea to the garden bench, with its time-worn wooden seat and the polished rust of its arm-rests.

Summer sun warmed him and he relaxed with a little smile, waiting for the longed-for visit, when he could soak up some of the excess energy that glowed out of his grandson, ten-year-old Sam.

To Conker Fear

Every year brings little fears
Of falling out of trees, and tears.
But doing it for love of conkers?
'You!' says Mum, 'you must be
bonkers!'

BARRY SEDDON

47

REPRINTED FROM ALAN RICK'S MEMOIRS; 'MY LIFE AND OTHER MISADVENTURES ISBN 978-1-326-60665-7

The Birthday Party

ALAN RICK

I suppose the children's birthday party is one of the earliest events that stay in the mind forever. These spectacles, organised as much for the parents themselves as for the children, made possible the display of the offspring in all their gaudy finery. It required the sort of lengthy and thorough preparation of the child that borders on the sadistic. The event I was dragooned into was the birthday of Janet, a little girl across the street. It seemed a slight enough cause to me considering the ordeal I was put through beforehand. This was to be scrubbed from head to foot, whiter than some peoples' doorsteps, to have my hair vandalised to reduce it to an acceptable length, to be decked out in clothes that I thought were only worn by dolls and to be on the receiving end of a moral lecture concerning manners, conduct and unattainable objectives. A small spirited boy was not meant for any of this I thought, as I glumly submitted to the strange preoccupations of the adult world. But perhaps the party itself would provide opportunities to sabotage it – we would see.

These parties followed a certain ritual – one shook the hand of Janet, with an air of feigned cordiality, and murmured a few words of courtesy, memorised from my mother's list drilled into me earlier that day.

The children, garbed as if at some exotic festival, were seated round a circular table eyeing the goodies, their eyes growing larger by the minute. Any attempt to touch any until the starting signal was firmly restrained by the parents, arranged like a circle of prison guards.

The parents had their own agenda in all of this, which was to secure two hours of peace and quiet while the children were engaged in the absorbing task of filling their faces. Nowadays this would be achieved by the irritating means of the Computer game. His or her room will be turned into a mass of wires and plugs and screens, the child will be wired up and plugged into about 40 controls worldwide and can spend the next two hours shouting at about three million children round the globe. Not in my day. At a party you just filled each child with about three times its weight in jelly, gave it a lump of play dough (then called Plasticine) and retired to put your feet up. Simple!

There was that wonderful moment during this party when Janet's mother, oozing maternal bliss from every pore, came round to each of us in turn with a large plate of cakes. At last, a reason for being here; grown-ups were not all wrath and finger wagging then and I had my fair share of greed. There were benefits in allowing the backs of your ears to be inspected and even your hair combed. At last the lady of the house approached me – this promised to be my lime-lit moment.

'And which cake would you like little Alan?' she gushed with a smile.

'The biggest.' I answered benignly.

My mother's face assumed the pallor of deep winter frost, the prison guards shifted uneasily and the laughter from the other children sounded like a gurgling drain.

Later that day at home the consequences were dire but not lasting. Would I try to sabotage adult morality again? No – the price was too high and, in any case I would have to join them one day.

Humpty Dumpty

AUDREY EDWARDS

Humpty Dumpty sat on a wall. Why?

Humpty Dumpty had a great fall. Serves him right, what was he doing up there in the first place?

Probably peering into the King's garden.

And all the king's horses and all the king's men; they're not completely blameless either, why are they involved?

I can't help myself. I have to find out why Humpty sat on the wall.

The reasons could be many.

Was the wall his Achilles heel?

Did he climb it just because it was there? That seems feasible.

But I like to think he was spying on the King. Why else would the King's men be after him?

What was the King up to that provoked such an interest?

Could there be a story here we are all missing?

I'll find out if it kills me.

Reward

ALAN RICK

She looked so forlorn – a little girl of about 7 years old – standing in front of the counter of a sweet shop, looking with eager expectation at the jars of sweets ranged along the shelves and the attractive display of chocolate on the counter. Hers was a modest request indeed – a

simple Kit Kat costing sixty-two pence.

'Could I have one of these please?' Her upturned eyes would have been enough to melt the snows of the Siberian Tundra.

She offered the money to the lady behind the counter who examined it with no particular sign of being melted – commercial interest won easy over romantic sentiment.

Here was a crisis – the money our little waif offered was six pence short of the required amount.

'You don't have enough money to pay for it,' said the shop assistant with uncalled-for abruptness.

The little girl's face assumed the saddest picture I had ever seen, her lip trembled and tears formed rivulets. What to do? I passed from my own pocket the price of the Kit Kat with the words, 'Give the girl the Kit Kat for goodness sake.'

This was done with what was at least a semblance of a sympathetic look from the other side of the counter.

Leaving the shop and some 10 yards further down the pavement I felt a tug of my coat from behind me. It was the little girl.

'This is yours,' she said, offering me the fifty-six pence she still had in the pocket of her dress.

'How is it mine?' I replied.

'You paid for the Kit Kat so this is yours,' she insisted.

'No. No. In fact here is another fifty pence to go with it – so now you are richer than you were this morning when you got up.'

I shall never forget that look of worship on her face as I went on my way. Some seek their reward in this life by accumulating material things – but there is a certain kind of reward that cannot be counted on those terms – I acquired some of it that day.

'I wish you were my Dad,' came the forlorn cry.

'But you have one already to be kind to you,' was my lame response.

'No – he hits my Mum.'

A 1940's Childhood

Sylvia Edwards

World War 2 was nearing its end as I emerged into the small mill town of Darwen, in the North West of England. Most of my childhood seemed happy. My dad had come back from the war unharmed. How lucky I was! Though I did not realise it then.

Here is one of my earliest memories. Imagine me, about four years old. I lie in bed, staring at a sliver of moonlight through the curtain. Again, I have been wakened by the banging. I know what it is and have got used to it. The hammering goes on - then stops. Dad opens the door of his work room next to the bedroom where my brother and I sleep. His large, shadowy figure creeps silently around us. Does he smile? I like to think so. Then I hear the door close softly, and his footsteps growing fainter as he goes downstairs. I drift back to sleep.

Why do I remember this? Because it was very special. Weeks later, on Christmas Day, after yet more hammering and banging, I realised what it was about. My father had been making me a doll's house. It was built of wood - all of it. Every piece had been crafted and shaped by him, even the tiny beds, the table and chairs. My mother, bless her, had made tiny curtains and bed covers.

It was the best Christmas present I had ever had; probably because it had been made by people I loved. I never wanted to give it away, even when, years later, I no longer played with it. That doll's house sat in my bedroom, taking pride of place, amongst all the paraphernalia of my teens. That same Christmas, Dad also made my brother a fort, again out of wood, with soldiers. I remember this time as an era of war games - played with toy guns and swords.

How did we play in those distant days? I was brought up in a small terraced house, very working class, but I can't remember going without things I needed. I say this because, so many years later, I can't believe how materialistic childhood has become. At birthdays and Christmas my grandchildren receive piles of presents that they open one after the other, the excitement seemingly in the pulling and tearing of wrapping paper, rather than in the joy of the gift itself. How would they react to just one or two simple toys, along with an apple and an orange in a Christmas stocking?

Kids today wonder what we did without phones, tablets and computers. But what wasn't there wasn't missed. I remember having fun outside whenever the weather allowed. Everyone in our street knew each other because we played out together. Remember those long skipping ropes at either side of the road? The older kids spun the rope for the younger ones. We played outside far more than children do today. But of course, we could, because very few cars came up our street. If one did - it was likely to be the doctor or somebody socially 'higher up' than we were. Any car parked on our street was a source of huge curiosity. We would peer through the windows, marvelling at this strange thing and wondering where the important person was going. Who was sick? What was the matter?

Some games haven't changed - tag, hide and seek, hopscotch and hula hoops, which my grandchildren still love. We played leap frog. The yoyo was also popular. We also had marbles, tiddlywinks and snakes and ladders. I remember juggling balls against the wall of our house.

The films of the day also influenced play. Boys became Cowboys and Indians, running around, whooping. The after-effects of the war were reflected in playful battles with pretend guns and weapons.

I played a lot with my dolls; taking them for walks and lifting them in and out of their baby carriage. My dolls lay on beautiful bedding, just like being in a portable bed. I also had a lovely, pink rag doll that was soft and squidgy; like a cuddly friend in bed.

Looking back, our toys seem simple compared with those of today. My dolls did not wee or cry. Cars were not remote: my brother pushed them along the floor with his hands and made the appropriate noises. Pan lids and wooden spoons did as drums. The games we played worked because we put our own sense of fun into them. Yet these simple things offered just as much pleasure as the most sophisticated tablets and devices available for our latest generation. Children had to be inventive and creative. Now, I ask, did we, much of the time, invent our own fun - because we had to? And did we learn to enjoy more - with less? I think we did.

Did the children of my day read more? I certainly read a lot. Most of my books were the classics, although only recently have I come to realise how long ago they were written: Heidi (Joanna Spyri 1881), Little Women (Louisa M Alcott 1869), Black Beauty (Anna Sewell). And of course, there was Enid Blyton: The Secret Seven and Famous Five. I remember these books as hardbacks with wrap-around paper covers. My books were precious and I read my favourite stories over and over. I also kept them for many years - eventually handing them down to my own children.

Annuals also appeared in many Christmas stockings. My brother had his Robin Hood Annuals, while I devoured the Film Star Annuals that depicted glamorous stars on the covers; again a reflection of the movie stars of the time (Doris Day, Audrey Hepburn).

Certainly, we played more socially than today's children. As I write, a 2017 TV News programme reports that many children arrive in nurseries and reception classes without the necessary language and social skills for learning. Alarm bells have been ringing for years in schools, as successive governments have fought to halt the decline of language and communication in our young children. Should we be alarmed at the modern obsession with mobile phones and screens? Are the negatives outweighing the positives? The machines are here to stay; developing and multiplying with alarming speed. While the clock cannot be rewound, we need to question where some of these technological trends are going and consider any unintended consequences.

There is hope! When our family members get together at weekends and Christmas, we play games, old and new. My five year old grand-daughter adores Snakes and Ladders. They still play hide and seek. Games make us laugh. So, long live 'games' as the foundation of family togetherness.

What did we watch on TV just after the war? I remember vaguely the first children's TV programmes: Muffin the Mule (about 1948). Muffin was a lovable puppet, handled by Annette Mills. I loved Andy Pandy, from the summer of 1950. A later favourite was Bill and Ben: the flower pot men, with Little Weed (1952) - three delightful garden characters, who came to life for us children when the gardener had gone in for his lunch. These, I later realise, were all part of the BBC Watch With Mother series (spin off from Listen with Mother), which I watched on the small black and white TV that sat in the corner of our living room.

How sexist we think it now! Watch with Mother indeed! Yet, many mothers in those days were at home all day with us children. Few nurseries then! Keeping house, shopping and caring for the family was the main role for most women : as it was for my mother. How things have changed!

Later, along came Sooty (1955), Rag, Tag and Bobtail (1953) - featuring Rag the Hedgehog, Tag the Mouse and Bobtail the Rabbit. Blue Peter came along in 1958, which I remember well although I was by then 13. Interestingly, Blue Peter has ended up as the longest-running children's TV show in the world.

It seems strange when I look at my grand-children; the 11 year old wanting to grow up before her time, ears pierced, wearing eye shadow and lipstick at weekends. Even at 13 and 14, I remember being far closer to childhood than I ever was to adulthood. Perhaps I was slower than some of my peers to take those first tentative steps into the adult world. I was clever enough (having passed the 11-Plus for grammar school), but hopelessly naive - about boys, about growing up, about the world. That naivety lasted a long time. Childhood for me, definitely lasted far longer than it did with my own children, and the children of today. Was that a good - or a bad thing, I wonder.

VENICE

What's New on the Rialto?

BILL CAMERON

'Ahoy there, Captain of the Dolabella.' The skipper of the coastal trader, Corona del Maris, called across the turbulent waves of the Aegean, 'Sail along with us for a spell. We're outbound from Venice for Trieste and have some news for you.'

Captain Hortensio of the merchantman, Dolabella, turned to his first mate.

'Mohammed,' he ordered, 'heave to alongside the Corona del Maris. I believe he has news for us from our home port that we need to learn.'

On the trader, Captain Henry Bosco leaned on the gunwale and called up.

'Is this one of the vessels of the merchant Antonio of Venice?'

'Aye, we are indeed one of the surviving few. Two of our fleet were lost passing through the Straits of Messina. Fortunately, the crews were able to land on Sicily and should have found a way home. But Antonio must be short of cash now with his investment in this endeavour. This trip has already taken over three months, but this cargo of oriental spices will soon fill his coffers.'

'Truly, he is in need of capital from your cargo and his debt stands him in peril of his Christian soul.'

'How so, Captain? Isn't my master's credit good on the island? I thought he was well funded. The last I heard he had advanced some three thousand ducats to his friend Bassanio – if the gossip we heard in Calicut is to be believed.'

Captain Bosco explained how the loan had been borrowed initially from an unscrupulous money lender and the debt was about to fall due. He went on to say that the earlier vessels should have returned in good time to repay the debt. In the case of the debt being unpaid, the generous and creditworthy friend would forfeit an outrageous penalty of a pound of his living flesh. Now Shylock, the mean moneylender, was anticipating a vengeful recompense for the anti-Semitic treatment that had been levied on him by traders during his time in Venice. He would extract a malicious retribution from the townsfolk in the person of the popular merchant, Antonio.

The master of the Dolabella thanked his informant and wished him a safe journey with full sails and then he turned to his mate, 'Mohammed, turn about and hoist full sail for Venice.'

Once under way, the first officer turned to his skipper, 'Sir, as a Muslim, I have no love for the Jewish race any more than you do, but I think you will agree that Shylock has been poorly treated. Do we need the danger of speed in hurrying back? Surely, he cannot insist on taking the life of Senor Antonio? Let us travel safely and give our ship-owner time to reflect on his oppression of the Jew.'

'Mohammed, we have sailed together many years and we accept each other for what we are. Nevertheless, I don't share your confidence that a suitable lawyer will be found in Venice and assure an equable resolution. I do believe that our master Antonio is in peril of his life. We will make all haste for Venice with our cargo.'

The journey in the heavily laden vessel took a further three days before they picked up the pilot at Venice Roads.

Keen for news, the master called to the pilot as he climbed the rope ladder, 'What news on the Rialto of my master Antonio?'

The pilot frowned, 'Not good when I left the court this morning. He will need a very good solicitor and the lightweight defender representing him doesn't inspire confidence. Did you know Shylock has taken the case before the Duke who is scrupulously fair and applies the literal word of the law?'

The captain commented, 'By the time we are tied up, I guess Shylock will have cashed in his surety. I fear that Antonio's life will be short or extinguished. And this tempest will not speed us to clear waters quickly.'

He scanned the sea gloomily.

The pilot, however, replied positively, 'We'll be clear of the rough sea once we round this headland. As soon as we pass the pier, we will be in the calmer water of the Grand Canal. Look, you can see the roof of the Doge's Palace already.'

As predicted, they were on the quayside very soon. News of their arrival had preceded them when the agent met the ship on the quayside. He was urgently interrogated by the vessel's master and reported that Antonio's new fiancée, Portia, had not only successfully defended him at the trial but reversed the penalty such that Shylock had forfeited his own fortune as the penalty for attempted murder.

In a bar on Dingle Road

In a bar on Dingle Road in Tralee

The Murphy clan met up for a spree

Downing whiskey and stout

Much merriment did spout

Their craic could silence a banshee.

ROSEMARY SWIFT

CROATIA

Krka Valley

CHRIS VICKERS

KRKA, having only the one vowel at the end, I was figuring how to pronounce the name of the valley we were scheduled to visit. It is, we found, K I R K A and rhymes with burqa.

However, place sounds are immaterial when one visits such a magical environment. Sir David Attenborough would be truly in his element!

The valley is a truly dramatic, magical place created by the River Krka flowing through a series of gorges before joining the sea. When first glimpsed, from high on a twisting, narrow mountain road the valley is a central, horse-shoe shaped island. One continues to get tantalizing peeks through the foliage as the road spirals downwards. Eventually we trundled down until we reached the ticket office and had a loo break before exploring nature's Disneyland.

As soon as one steps from the vehicle there is a beautiful, cool, perfumed freshness to the air. That's due to the fact that the valley is watered by seventeen waterfalls, growing ever more imposing and culminating in a giant fall creating a large lake in which people swim and by which they sunbathe, relax and eat ice creams.

At the beginning one walks along regular roads past quiet, shaded ponds which are home to shoals of static, black fish, hovering as they feed. There's an old wood mill for those inclined to visit it. But as we ventured on the air is filled with sonic-like booming croaks and strain our eyes to eventually spot fat-bellied frogs, sitting on reeds and old roots, bellowing raucously at each other.

The nostrils now inhale an earthy smell as the babbling water gushes over gnarled tree roots, green fronds dip and trail into the water, alongside waving green reeds and algae; fast flowing water agitates the muddy stream bed. Ears are filled with the sounds of gurgling water, birdsong and the loud, endless croaking of the bullfrogs. The colours are greens, browns, greys and black combinations from the ancient trees as old as time and still standing sentry.

The wardens at KRKA have constructed a wooden circular platform which leads you through the waterfalls and past the differing streams and mini lakes and right in nature's way. It is relaxing and reinvigorating to be at one with nature like this.

The experience is intense and the sights, sounds and smells almost literally intoxicating. There's a constant wash-day freshness as the water rushes through, cleansing and rejuvenating all in its wake.

As one walks on along the platform the sights and sounds and colours vary as yet another waterfall feeds in more water and nature gouges and moulds the landscapes. We completed the lap of the platform and lunched near the big 'fall and the lake. Happy to have been immersed in nature for the day but also sorry that it was over. Like the thrill of a rollercoaster, you crave to relive the experience.

Stone Ages

One in each hand I hold stones from the ages.

One moulded by fire, the other by ice

One found on a hillside on which I was walking

One on a shoreline, a gift from the sea.

The grey one is pumice from mother earth's cauldron

Boiling for centuries down in the dark

The ice of a glacier carried the other

Smoothed it to velvet, then gave it to me.

It's many long years since I found them

They'll be here long after I die

Treasured for most of my lifetime,

To the earth .... a mere blink of an eye.

BARRY SEDDON

`CUBA`

Dagger in the Dust

BILL CAMERON

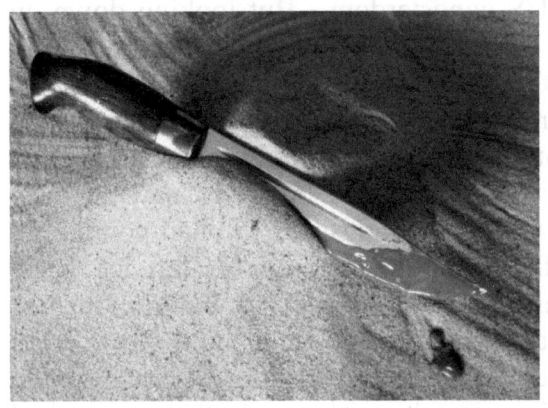

Jack Schulz peered down on the bloodied and muddied corpse. 'Joe Stassi ain't gonna like this one bit,' he said to himself as he took another stick from his second pack of Luckies of the day.

Havana in the late 50s was OK if one – you were already bad, two – you were 'in' with the Batista government or three – you didn't give a damn. Schulz fell into the last category after leaving Chicago with the lipstick of Blanche Beauregard on his collar and the dogs of Jimmy 'Razor' Rockwell on his tail. Times with the long-legged, peroxide blonde Blanche had been fast and exciting but necessarily brief. She belonged to Rockwell and was not going to give up the penthouse lifestyle for a jobbing private eye like Schulz. It was a long way and a long time from Chicago to Cuba and Rockwell was never going to bigger than the likes of Meyer Lansky, particularly now the more illustrious associates Lucky Luciano and Bugsy Seigel were no longer on the scene. Yes, Schulz was OK for now but he still needed an income to maintain his liquor intake. He had no reservation when one of Joe Stassi's henchmen invited him to 'Keep an eye on this guy,

Roberto, and let me know what he does – especially if he starts to get pally with any of Trafficante's hoods.'

Schulz told himself it would be a simple job for an investigator who was already keeping under the radar. It was both legal and as safe as anything in the violent and corrupt world of hotels and casinos shared amongst Batista and precariously balanced US gangsterdom. But looking down on the bloodied corpse of Roberto, a slam-dunk of fear hit the pit of his stomach – and there was nowhere to run from this job. He could not at the moment afford the luxury of a plan – just go into detective auto-pilot as he had been told at the academy and see where it leads. His eyes scanned the body. He saw the deep and flaming laceration where the gangster's life had poured out of a gaping slash of the femoral artery on his left leg. His experience reminded him that this had led to unconsciousness and death. An identical wound on the right thigh shouted the blood-letting was deliberate. The sadistic killer wanted Roberto to die with time to reflect on why. The trail of blood tracked back round the corner of an adobe built barn – occasional pools in the dust showed where the victim had paused on his agonising, exhausting trek. Spurts of arterial red on the dirt confirmed that Roberto had begun with a strong pounding heart.

Behind the barn, he could not fail to see the neat dais of dirt composed to exhibit a six inch blood-smeared dagger. Clearly the weapon had been withdrawn to leave the wound open once the arteries had been severed.

The assassin wanted everyone to know his cruel intent and to send some kind of message to someone.

With another Lucky Strike filling his lungs, he sat on the wall to think. Questions spun in the detective's brain. Who was saying what and to whom? More difficult because he didn't know where this guy Roberto fitted in the gambling scene. Was he a major or minor player? Did he run a joint or a book or was he merely a runner for one of the big fish?

The co-operation amongst gangland chiefs in Havana was tenuous and relied on mutual distrust and a balance of power that favoured none over any other. Like the recently branded 'cold war', the lid was kept on this local Cuban version by a mutually assured annihilation. But had someone blinked? He listed the candidates who were all possible perpetrators and victims simultaneously. Albert 'Mad Hatter' Anastacia had recently been snooping into his investments in the Bandes cartel, managed by Lansky. He was reported to be very dissatisfied with his partners. But he had been mown down in the barber shop by a mob hit in October of '57, which Stassi was said to be behind. Maybe Roberto had something on the Sans Souci nightclub owner, Santos Trafficante? He had been mentioned by Stassi's lieutenant in the detective's instructions after all. He could be worth silencing forever by either side.

A thought floored Schulz, 'What if the hit had been ordered by his employer, Stassi's gopher – or even Stassi himself? But what was the message of the dagger in the dirt?'

Then he considered the other massive piece of the murderous crooked jigsaw puzzle. Could the government of President Fulgencio Batista be involved? The President was allegedly taking up to 30 cents on every dollar profit from the mob's casinos. He could easily arrange for the police or army to take out any individual with impunity. The question kept returning 'But why Roberto?' On the other hand, Roberto, a native Hispanic, possibly Cuban, could be spying for Batista. The sleuth was missing something. He had to find out more about Roberto.

Nothing else could be discovered from the site, but he didn't want the local police following the trail too soon, so pocketed the dagger and kicked over the pile of dirt. Anyone poking around now will only see another gangland killing. No big deal in a city swarming with American criminals.

He opened the rickety door of his downtown apartment. He couldn't get used to the superfluous key. If he fixed the lock today it would be broken again tomorrow – and what did he have to steal anyway? The smell of cheap scent – lots of it – hit his nostrils, overwhelming the stale concoction of cigarettes and bourbon. A dark-skinned, raven-haired dream lay sprawled across the mattress that passed as a bed. Sure, she was dressed, but the fit of her clothes was tight in all the right places. Every contour, mound and hollow was a perfect complement to the sparkling teeth and brilliant green eyes that smiled a welcome you would never expect from a stranger. For a moment Roberto was no more a problem now than Blanche Beauregard back in the windy city. When he bent to loosen his shoe laces, the dagger reminded him of the urgent matter. He hoped a few phone calls would clear the air somewhat. He had to put her on the back burner to smoulder for a while – and couldn't she smoulder?

'Hi,' he said, 'ain't this heat unbearable? I don't know what you want but I'll need to wash, shave and put on some clean clothes. Can I meet you in the bar in, say, half an hour?'

'You need not freshen up on my account, senor,' she said. Then, trembling: 'I don't think it's wise to go back out of the door just now.'

A crash of splintered door accompanied the bullet that whistled past his ear and buried itself into the crumbling plaster wall. The door hit the floor as a swarthy six-footer strode into the room then pinned Schulz to the floor.

A thick Spanish voice spoke through garlic breath that could be carved like meatloaf.

'Why have you sabotaged our message, gringo?'

'I don't know what you mean. I've got enough problems already so whatever you want from me, take it and go. Here's my wallet for what it's worth.' He reached in his pocket and felt the dagger. Did he feel confident in this position? No. Life was the preferable option. But he did not get the chance to use the knife. His wrist was twisted by the stronger man and the knife fell to the floor. The intruder picked it up and smiled.

'One day, Senor, you will remember your part in the revolution. The day is coming when the Batista regime and its imperialist Yankee collaborators will no longer rob my country of its wealth while the real Cubans live in poverty. You may have removed the symbol this time, but more will die and the world will recognise the dagger in the dirt and the slow bleeding death as an icon of our fight against the tyrants who have bled Cuba for so long. Even as we speak, our leaders Fidel and Che are building the revolutionary army that will march on Havana and drive out the imperialist Yankees and traitor Batista. Remember these names, senor. They will soon be on the lips of the world.'

Schulz looked over the rebel's shoulder and caught the girl's smile. He could be staying in Cuba for some time. His brain went into positive overdrive.

He addressed the revolutionary, 'Is there room in the revolution for a run-down honest American? With my experience in the army motor pool maybe I could work on your ordnance vehicles.

'There are also thousands of US-made Dodges, Buicks, Plymouths, Cadillacs, Chevrolets and other bat-winged motors which will need maintaining later. Yes, I think I have a contribution to make to the revolution.'

Toogoolawahs

Ashen black, grey and white
The dust of devastation all around
Conflagration gone and out of sight
Wisps of smoke no fauna there to make a sound

Toogoolawah's pain and trial nears its end.
Flames no more to dance and play.
Orange lines of black top flames. skyward send.
Move away to change the forest green to grey.

Day and night the battle lines run.
A bastion against the all-consuming wall.
Trying to stem the work of summer's remorseless sun.
Eucalyptus and Bunyas overwhelmed stand blackened and tall.

Warm winds swirl and caress, flames their constant companion.
Always there to help its flamboyant friend.
A cacophony of wind and flame, in their ambulant abandon.
Surely nature's destructive gyrations must be near their end.

Dark clouds race across the pitiable scene.

Pitter patter welcomes the absentee rain.

Ash and steam heaven bent, water clear and clean.

Sent to cool the land and ease it's pain.

Time goes on as time must do.

The bush land awakens to the gentle rain.

The flora and fauna start anew.

To wait the season of fire again.

JOHN HASSALL

CROATIA

Mostar

CHRIS VICKERS

Listed on the itinerary on a recent holiday to Croatia was a trip to Mostar, famous for its bridge and closely associated with the savage fighting and ethnic cleansing featured during the Balkan conflicts of the 1990s. Indeed, scars from the terrible battles are still apparent beyond the cobbled lanes of the restored Ottoman quarter.

Founded in 1452 Mostar is a city and municipality in Southern Bosnia and Herzegovina, inhabited by some 106 thousand people, and is the most important city in the Herzegovina region, being the cultural capital and the centre of the Herzegovina-Neretva canton of the Federation. It was once Europe's border with the Ottoman Empire, and there remains a palpable sense of excitement and the mystery of East meeting West to this day.

We enjoyed a pleasant lunch at a restaurant perched above the River Neretva offering birds eye view of the iconic bridge with its rebuilt medieval towers - the originals having been blasted apart in 1993 in the war. As we ate, every so often a figure would dive from the bridge into the rock-strewn river far below to applause and cheers from the thronged tourists.

As we enjoyed our lunch we could see the young men whipping up a crowd and canvassing contributions, teasing them by pretending to dive only to pull back at the last minute in an effort to maximise interest and money. Having strutted and peacocked until satisfied, they were receiving their due worth. They then courageously launched themselves like Elvis Presley in the film Blue Hawaii.

The bridge is thus a hugely congregated place as tourists look on agog and locals try to move about their daily business. The cobbles of the narrow, steeply humped road have been worn shiny by generations of footfall and are lethal, so you are dodging people and concentrating on your footing at the same time as trying to move on.

The road's official name is Kujundzilak but is more romantically known as Gold Alley on account of the numerous traders and trinket sellers plying their trade along the route, with eager tourists checking out their wares. As you weave in and out of the masses there's a real buzz and a sense of straying into a different culture. However, as you progress away from the bridge, things calm down somewhat and calm and peace become the prevalent features.

Along the steep banks of River Neretva, with an elevation of 60m, and opposite the restaurant where we lunched, can be seen brightly coloured, beautiful houses. As one takes in the wider view several mosques rake the sky, alongside which are situated clusters of plain white humble homes.

Now, as we turn to walk back, the view is dominated by a large verdant hill, offering a different view of the bridge and flowing river. Another not-to-be-missed photo-op!

Although our trip lasted merely a day, Mostar captured the imagination; a melting pot of counter-cultures, exciting, vibrant and memorable.

SOUTH AMERICA

Firebird

BARRY SEDDON

Out of the sky it came, short of wing and loud of voice, like no bird we had ever seen. Its voice was like thunder. It shook the ribs and made the stomach a quaking drum

My people called it salamander, because it was always reborn on a blazing tail of fire, vanishing behind one of our hills and returning from behind another, rising fast, riding its flame, as loud and frightening as before.

One day it laid an egg that fell to earth and vanished in noise and smoke and fire that left a hole where our homes had been.

And soon we had to leave, because when we had buried our dead and rebuilt our village, the salamander returned with more birds of its clan and destroyed our world for ever.

BALKANS

Sylvia

Let me tell you a tale about Sylvia,

taught mathematics in Yugoslavia

she taught them to add,

to subtract and divide,

now one country no more – it is Serbia, - Montenegro,
Kosovo, Slovenia, Macedonia, Croatia, Bosnia and
Herzegovina.

BILL CAMERON

AUSTRALIA

Mooral *(Aboriginal for plenty)*

As the gentle curtains of soft spring rain, sweep their moisture laden tassels across the long parched bush, erasing winter's drought and resetting the cycle of life.

Bunya, eucalypts and palm begin their frantic growing rush, to invigorate and replenish a sorely depleted bush.

A yearly game of push and shove, nature's roulette wheel of strife, turning endlessly presenting death and glorious life.

The warm winds gently caress the now expectant buds, prompting an explosion of green , as leaves begin to sprout in a fevered springtime rush.

Insects free themselves from winters chrysalis tomb, bush turkeys call and display strutting with purposeful intent to out-compete the rest.

Crimson rosellas, green lorikeets and yellow sunbirds, search for materials far and wide ,to build this season's nest.

Flowers blossom, colours everywhere, nature's bountiful banquet of pollen and nectar made for all to share.

Huntsmen, orb-webs and geckos, always on the look out, nectar feeders patiently waiting to snare.

Generations come and generations go, the endless circle of life revolves around Mother Earth and her bountiful nurturing care.

JOHN HASSALL

The Visitor

BARRY SEDDON

One fine August afternoon in 1938, Alan Newman came to Emberswood, bearing strangeness on his shoulders like a cape of silk. Light and easy, he stepped down from the train onto our neat platform, a small dove-grey case in his yellow-gloved hand, nodded slightly, then stood serene, smiling faintly, as he gazed at the floral delicacy of our little station.

The train that brought him echoed his smooth confidence. No hiss of steam shivered the summer air as it slid away, almost silent.

Sean Fletcher, our station master for many years, shivered every time he recalled it. 'That train just wasn't right. Smooth and round it was, like a big silver worm. I swear it made no smoke, and it left like a bullet. No bang though, just a low hum - like my bees at twilight.

'Couldn't see a driver. There was only one carriage as well and no other passengers -- none I could see, anyway. The windows were odd, small and round and the glass was sort of milky-bright as though there was a funny light inside. I reckon it was probably a test engine, being tried out on a quiet day. Definitely not on the time-table. Very odd.'

Sean had started to say something. But the visitor had smiled, nodded politely and left, light-footing onto the sleepy street. We didn't know it, of course, but our little town was dreaming away another innocent summer on the road to war.

No-one recalls seeing Alan Newman on his way to the Sherwood Arms. Sean remembered a pale blue jacket, almost white trousers and light-weight black and white shoes, so he certainly should have been noticed. But the only other person to see our visitor was Maggie, the Sherwood's live-in receptionist and barmaid -- and that wasn't for long.

What she remembered most was his eyes – 'bright, glowing, almost purple,' she said. 'He sort of drifted in and booked to stay the night. His voice was soft and drifty as well, like wood smoke. He smelt like nutmeg. I told him he could eat at 6.30, but he said no, he'd brought his own food, would be leaving early and needed no breakfast. It was amazing how smooth he moved, like he was on ice-skates.'

Maggie, the main source of town gossip, was naturally keen to know more. During a quiet spell at the bar she slipped upstairs with a tray, a tumbler and a two-pint jug of cool water.

Alan Newman reacted very fast when she tapped at his door. It opened just a little, and before she could say a word, the smoky voice said that yes, thank-you, water was very welcome. Then, gloveless now, a slim, pale hand reached out and took the jug. Maggie, surprised and a little shaken, was turning to leave with the tumbler and tray when she heard water being gulped.

'It lasted less than a minute,' she said. 'Then the door opened again and out came the jug, empty.'

Maggie came on duty early the next day. There was no sign of her guest, but on the reception counter was a plain grey envelope. Inside was a generous payment: two crisp £5 notes, with a faint smell of nutmeg.

They weren't our usual black and white fivers. They were bluey-green, quite small, almost slippery, and bearing a picture of a lady wearing a crown. She must have been a queen, because   E II R was printed beside the portrait. And there was a section like a little window that you could see through. The biggest surprise however was the printed date -- 2016. They would not be useable for 80 years.

There was something else in the envelope -- a thin flexible disc bearing a printed message: *Tap lightly to play. Tap again to stop.* We tapped it and a spoken message in that drifty, smoky voice hung on the air like magic: 'Thank-you for being so kind. Perhaps we shall meet again, some day, some year.' We seldom play the message these days. We wrote down the words because the sound was getting fainter with each tap.

It is our very own secret, hidden away, never to be given up to some desk-bound official.

Our local headmaster says Mr Newman must have been a time-traveller. We hope he is right, because some of our children's children might one day meet him, shake his small pale hand and smell the nutmeg. Some day. Some year.

SWitCH

Time

Times to come and times long gone, they twine around our lives

Stonehenge shadow, mark on candle, gong,

Measured swing of pendulum and Indian summer days,

Kiss-me-quicks at Blackpools here-and-gone

Marks deep-scratched by weary convicts, serving out their time,

Measurements of lives beyond control

Not like the lovely bygone days when seasons softly blended

And country bells told farmers when to mow

Instead we have to fall beneath the clenching fists of clocks

Our castles cannot always be defended

Relentless time will keep forever ticking off the hours

Until the day when every watch is ended

BARRY SEDDON

Tomorrow's Ghosts

BARRY SEDDON

No worries; good to go; AOK; no prob. All the clichés. Familiar words to dull the edges of fear. And we are afraid. After all, we will be the first time-travellers.

Tomorrow is Tuesday. Before sunrise, we will be launched into next week. If the Sender fails to bring us back, with a newspaper to confirm the trip, only the lab-boys will know. We'll be gone forever and no families will miss us – we were recruited with that in mind.

And no, they wouldn't be able to wait a week, then come and find us. Think about it: while the boffins are waiting for next Tuesday, Mike and I will already be living onwards into the never-when, out of their reach forever. As untouchable as ghosts – time ghosts.

Our trip is Top Secret because it won't be for scientific glory, but to give our benighted Kingdom a military edge. If it succeeds, our soldiers will be able to lay traps for the enemy. Like Usain Bolt sprinting out of sight around the bend and laying land-mines for the following runners. Cruel, but can war ever be kind?

As usual, Mike is pessimistic. "Easy for them to say it's safe! What about that poor bloody monkey? They brought it back alright. Dead!"

"Oh, come on Mike," I say. "That was last year. We'll be time pioneers. In all the history books, like Armstrong."

Mike changes tack. "What about that story where a time traveller steps on a butterfly and that one little change snowballs

81

into disaster? We could leave a trail of destruction. Who's to say?"

With Mike in this frame of mind there's only one thing for it. I buy another pint. Within an hour we're sleeping. Tomorrow's a big day.

Tuesday October 17 2038, is grey and misty, an anonymous sort of day. We are launched from a hidden cave by a shielded signal from our secret lab in Hayfield. The trip is no problem, just a slight dizziness and there we are. The cave looks no different. It wouldn't, of course – it's the same cave, thousands of years old ... plus a week.

Our journey by local bus into Whaley Bridge is uneventful. We rent a hotel room. Nothing seems different. No suspicious looks. After all, it's only next week.

Only next week! Time-talk is so confusing. Good old past, present and future from now on...

We never made the return trip. Some glitch in the Sender I suppose. Typically, Mike was disappointed. Not that we were stranded, but that he had turned out to be not quite right.

But we accepted it – no other option. And once we had, we searched for clues, just to tidy up the niggling loose ends. We needn't have bothered. In Hayfield it was as though the time-lab had never been. An old factory stood there, its brickwork flaking, paint long-gone. A report in the local newspaper said that on the day of our "arrival" there had been a slight earth tremor, but the only damage had been a couple of slates falling from the old factory roof.

So here we are "in the future," settling in. You can blend in very well in six months. We're still in Whaley Bridge. It's a pleasant little town, easy to put down roots and become part of the community. Mike is working at an electronic security company, and has married a local girl called Gillian after a whirlwind romance. I'm in the same company's labs, on the way to an advanced maths degree at the Open University. I've fallen for a librarian called Margaret and we marry next month.

I said Mike was not right in his dire predictions. Lately I've been almost wishing he was. For there is a dark side.

Margaret and I were chatting after a meal and the subject of time travel came up. She'd been filing some monthly science volumes at the library and been fascinated by a just-published study.

Time travel was just not possible, she declared. I was smiling to myself until she told me the study team's reasons: "The bottom line is that as everyone knows, nature abhors a vacuum and fills the gap. They say it has to be the same with time. It would be OK at the point of departure. A person travelling forward in time would leave a gap and a baby would be born that would otherwise have died.

"OK so far, but the rest of it isn't so nice, because at the time traveller's destination, someone would have to die to make room. Isn't that awful? Course, that's only if time travel is possible. The boffins don't think it is and I agree. Nature would never be so cruel, would it?"

I shivered. The subject has not come up again and I'm glad. Who died to make room for us?

Back of the Couch

BILL CAMERON

In 2097 the 'Mars Experiment' was abandoned. Forty seven years on the red planet had achieved nothing economically or scientifically. The cost of maintaining an outpost of forty to sixty humans had proved unjustifiable, despite the wide range of talents and temperaments. Even as an attempt at international cooperation it had worked only spasmodically. Earth-centred political ideologies of thirty seven nations seldom coalesced into any agreed serious target. Limits on personal baggage generally dictated an uncomfortable austerity over the contracted minimum term of five years. Rest and relaxation allowances permitted some 'home comforts', although shipping costs running to thousands of dollars per gram reduced the choices. Similarly expensive return flights prohibited repatriation and 'space junk' does not only float around the empty void of interplanetary vacuum. Man's footprint on Mars was therefore considerable when the station was abandoned and the planet allowed to resume its dead status towards the end of the 21st century.

Fortunately, over the following millennia, the sands and red dust of the lifeless planet buried the settlement in its sheltered crater and a passing astronaut would be hard pressed to see that man had ever trod a clumsy boot on the surface. The sole exception was one individual's 'home comfort' which took the form of an inflatable two-seater couch in the super-lightweight graphene material. The featherweight sofa fabricated in heat resistant material was blown undamaged out of the crater when the final rocket blasted off the surface.

It was discovered on the surface by an exploratory drone from across the universe, four thousand years later. By remarkable coincidence this vessel had been launched from a remote corner of the universe at about the same time as man was leaving Mars. Travelling at five percent of the speed of light the alien vessel had taken four millennia to cross the void in search of other life forms from the planet Notthemus. The drone had collected the now deflated couch and relayed its first report on the advanced material, indicating to the alien intellect an intelligent life form. Then the conundrums commenced. Like armchairs and comfortable furniture the world over, there is always a collection of *'things that have fallen down the back of the settee'*.

These artefacts could not have been within the memory banks of the alien drone, so were arranged, photographed in 3-D, X-rayed, UV-scanned and details transmitted back to the home planet at the speed of light.

It was still 200 years before the message arrived home. Advanced scientific knowledge and thousands of years cultural development were, nonetheless, incapable of recognising a domino, a piece of jigsaw and a pair of knitting needles.

To this day, The Museum of Interplanetary Exploration has the items on display with the challenge, 'What was the message the Martians left for us with these things? Who made these artefacts and what were they used for?'

Speculation, ranging over generations, has arrived at a consensus opinion that the inhabitants of the dead planet of Mars made tools and used them with two hands, evidenced by the knitting needles. The jigsaw piece declaimed that Martians were sophisticated

in the arts, producing irregular-shaped, coloured artworks with aesthetic appeal rather than exact photographic references. And in the more prosaic minds there was a keen appreciation of the symmetry manifest in a double four domino.

The Notthemus race regretted the disappearance of such an advanced civilisation on Mars and turned its attention to a totally different sector of the universe, leaving Earth and Mars in the backwaters of space-time for eternity.

Janus

BARRY SEDDON

She orbits the Sun, oh so close she circles him. Men have named her Mercury, but others have nicknamed her Janus, because she has two faces.

One of them, where iron boils, stares into solar fury, locked in that direction by the changeless rules of gravity. On her other face, even quicksilver freezes, as she gazes forever outwards across the frigid light years.

Janus has siblings, but they dance far away in an unconcerned gavotte: red-robed Mars, silver-clad Venus, blue-gowned Earth, lovely Saturn in her rainbow bolero.

From her distant side-line, eternally lonely, Cinderella Janus looks past them into the abyss.

Black Mill

BARRY SEDDON

Pete did not sleep well that night. He had joined the local history club and one of the first speakers had explained how an empty local mill gained its shivery nickname -- Black Mill.

It stemmed back to the early 1900s when weaving was still in full swing. During building work in the mill's cobbled entrance yard, a digger had unearthed a mass-grave, full of hundreds of little bones.

It was the last resting place of dozens of under-age children. Their parents, poverty-stricken and desperate, had sent them there to work. Many of them, already under-nourished and sickly, had died in the harsh conditions and the bosses had buried them in the mill-yard to escape the law.

That was a cold, dark time, but Pete's insomnia had been triggered on a warm autumn evening. From spring onwards, a record-breaking summer had shed rain only in the time before dawn and the nations of the earth had taken a breath and put war aside for a while.

As perfect days were fading through a gentle time that seemed to be lasting forever, four men and their wives were chatting quietly at the brass-railed bar of their local pub, while girls at tables in shadowed alcoves were murmuring sweet-nothings to their young men.

Jack had just told a little joke about his factory foreman and Pete had ordered fresh drinks, when Jimmy Frith came in. Pale, sweating, breathing hard, glancing over his shoulder a little fearfully, he closed the door and leaned his back to it as though barring entry to a demon.

When Frank and Pete reached him, he was muttering over and over about some very strange goings on at Black Mill. They got him to the bar, Joe dragged a stool up and put a pint in his hand, then the four pals and their wives waited for him to calm down.

Finally, Jimmy drew a deep shuddery breath and said, in a steady voice more effective than any rant: "I've always said there's something weird about that mill. You walk past, even in full sunshine, and it sort of broods at you. Perhaps it's coz it's so big and so empty." He shivered. "Pete knows what I mean, don't you mate?"

Pete nodded. He had worked at the mill all his life, from being a lad sweeping lint from the weaving shed corners, right through to retiring. He'd even spent a few months as a night watchman, until the echoing  emptiness drove him out. The huge weaving rooms, the dank weft cellars and rust-scabbed looms, hunched over like dying witches, had lingered in his dreams for a while, but they'd finally gone.

Jimmy was ending his tale. "I was passing the mill on my way here," he said. "It started with a simple thing, certainly nothing to be scared of. There I was, looking forward to a pint and a chat, when I heard this little tapping noise.

"I looked around. Tap-tap-tap. Nothing. Tap-tap-tap, just a weak little sound, almost scratchy. Then I looked upwards and saw them. At a first-floor window, two little white hands were tapping at the glass. Tapping, tapping. Then they waved and vanished. I ran all the way here."

As the women squealed and the men shook their heads in puzzlement, Pete smiled wryly to himself. He liked Jimmy, enough to take his mate's outrageous tales with a pinch of salt. Anyway, Jimmy's super-fibs were in a totally different league to his and at school it had been fun watching a master at work, while his audience wriggled in a delicious listening fever.

Jimmy hadn't told any super-fibs lately, so out of kindness to his friend on the night of the little white hands, Pete didn't give the game away. The group was subdued however – even the usually gossipy wives were quieter than usual -- and the session broke up early.

Pete walked home with Jimmy as the sky's last camp fires were dying in the west. Still believing that his friend had resurrected his tall story habit, he said so, laughed and told him he'd scored a definite ten out of ten.

For a moment Jimmy was silent, then said quietly, "I wasn't fibbing, Pete. It happened just like I said. I hope we all sleep well tonight."

After a restless night, still haunted by Jimmy's story, and the grisly history lecture, Pete found a note on the mat from the old lady next door. Could he please pop round to the newsagents at the end of Mill Street and sort out a bill she'd forgotten to pay? It wasn't far, was it? She said. He could take the short cut past the mill.

Pete thought briefly about the brooding shell of Black Mill and went the long way round.

Mirror Image

BARRY SEDDON

I went on the pull once too often. Jane found out, greeted me with two packed suitcases and I walked down the path and out of her life. She started dealing with me via a solicitor. I hadn't the energy to contest it.

At work I moped around, sold half the expected number of cars, and one day there was something extra with my pay – my cards.

How fast the downward spiral turns! I can afford better but can't be bothered, so I live in a two-star B and B and eat in supermarket caffs for company. I'm lonely. I like girls and the pleasures they bring. But whether it's between the sheets or with pub company, the purpose is always the same – to ease the emptiness. I don't even have to talk. Sitting. Watching. Listening. The warm presence of people is enough.

Jack Marston, one of my salesman mates, pulled me from the brink. He walked into Tesco's one night and saw me brooding over skinned-over coffee. He dragged me out, physically dragged me out, took me home, ignored my excuses for the state of the room, got me changed and spruced and brought me to this place.

Bar None. A little club, recently opened, and still smelling new. Lots of tables, with couples, foursomes, friends, lovers. At the bar, girls and single blokes like me, greeting others or chatting with the staff. Easy-on-the-eye lighting and -- most important – a murmuring of voices. People just being there, keeping emptiness at bay.

Jack got me settled at the bar, gave me an old-fashioned look, hinted at a car sales vacancy down the road and left me to it

So, on a trendy swivel stool, all chrome and fake leather, I sit here in blazer, slacks and fine-knit roll-neck, pretending to be young and relaxed. Forty-eight years old and counting.

Never mind that! I glance around, cheering up a bit, sussing out my new-found company. Mustn't be seen staring, though. Behind the bar is a long, bronze-tinted mirror. That's it! Perfect for seeing without being seen.

I'm disappointed. Nothing to write home about with this lot. Most of the tables, fake marble on cast iron legs, are occupied by courting couples, women with Radley handbags exchanging posh gossip; groups of loud and hearty blokes, obediently laughing at the jokes their alpha males are telling; haughty young girls with retinues of even younger men, stumbling through the mazy ways of the mating game.

I sigh, about to give up, when something impossible begins. In the mirror, at one of the tables, I can see three women talking and laughing. The fourth chair is empty.

The reflection is not too clear. I blink to re-focus and in that moment, there is a fourth person at the table. Not just settling down but there. There's something oddly familiar about him, like someone seen in a dream. He's probably in his late forties, with a long, vertically-creviced face and wearing a heavy black overcoat, what used to be called a London Fog. He isn't really old, but somehow, he seems ancient.

An undertaker on his day off perhaps... That would explain his distant look, emotionless and cool, and the way he's so relaxed, just sitting and listening. I'd give anything to be like that. Even so, where did he suddenly appear from? It's all a bit creepy.

Now I notice something even more strange. He is being totally ignored. I mean, totally. He might as well be invisible. One of the three women, youngish and blonde, is waving her arms about and comes very close to hitting his face. Another

91

turns and laughs towards him, loud and long. Neither makes him even flinch.

The mirror is not perfect. Maybe I'm imagining things. I swivel round to see the real thing. The man in black has vanished. No, he hasn't! He now sits, still unflinching, at a table a fair distance from the first, where three loud-mouth city types are stuffing their faces with free olives.

Must have been mistaken. Trick of the light perhaps. I turn back to my drink, glancing at the mirror. This time he's really gone, not at any of the tables. I'm beginning to be worried – almost frightened.

I signal the bartender for another drink but, as bartenders often do, he ignores me. Irritated, I signal again, wave in fact, to make sure. Still he ignores me and I stand to go. They'll not see me again! Don't like the place anyway. Something wrong about it.

As I turn, I'm briefly looking at the mirror. My own reflection has gone. Shaken, I look again at the real room and drop back a step. The man in black is walking rapidly towards me, smiling properly at last. There's nowhere to go. I'm leaning back against the bar, trapped and quite afraid. Now we are face to face and I realise how alike we are.

He says nothing, but puts out his hand. In trembling reflex, I reach out and grasp it. It's cool and dry. We shake hands. He pulls me towards him, nose to nose. I can feel his breath. I breathe it in and he disappears.

Something inside tells me I'll never again feel alone

.

Under the Clock

Sylvia Edwards

'Where are we going?'

'On a train journey - you like trains, don't you, Alice?'

'Yes, but ... where are we going on the train?' the child persisted.

'You'll see.'

10.30 am. Jane bought the tickets then took her daughter's hand and sat her down on the bench to wait. Here it was, on time, exactly to the minute. Just like last year! And the year before that. And the year before... She gazed down at her child's blonde curls. Where had the time gone? Alice would be five in September. Jane clenched her fists as the train rumbled noisily into the station. March! How she hated that month! If only she could forget. March 12th - Sunday. She had been clasping her special secret to her heart - longing to tell him. That secret - threatening to burst out - but she had forced herself to wait for the right moment. When they reached the hotel. But then ... too late. Jane shook the twisted thoughts from her head, causing her long hair to fly violently around as if a strong wind had suddenly caught it. Enough!

They boarded the train and settled into a seat with a table. Jane took out crisps and orange juice for Alice and watched her child switch on her iPad. She smiled as Alice lost herself in the adventures of Peppa Pig. And thought again about why she had come .... as the train gathered speed and fields whizzed past as if seen through the thrill of a fairground ride. If only this was... She closed her eyes for a moment as a strange nausea rose up from her stomach and threatened to erupt. Breathe slowly. It was going to be okay! He will be there ... again ... under the clock. Just as before.

'Mummy?' Will I have a Daddy one day?' Jane's stomach lurched as Alice's blue eyes locked onto hers ... as if the child was about to see right through her mother's lies.

'You do have a Daddy ... He had to ... go away.'

'When is he coming home? Doesn't he ever want to see us?'

'Soon ... and yes ... of course, he wants to see us – 'specially you.'

'Melanie's Daddy comes home every day.'

'Has Peppa finished already? Let's find you a different game.'

Jane felt her eyes well up as she fiddled with the iPad. Life wasn't fair! But she wasn't being fair either! To herself ... or to Alice. Then she thought about Phil. Why hadn't she told him? Dear Phil! There he was always there in the background of her life - yet ready, she knew, to move into a more prominent role. Hadn't he said so? She smiled. They got on so well. He was gentle ... funny ... and understanding. But surely he would only be patient for so long - then he would be gone and it would be her own fault. She could love him, if only ... Phil had wanted to take them both out today but she had made an excuse. Said she wasn't well. Lied!

The train was slowing. 11.50. Jane's heart began to race. No longer was she afraid. Hadn't she placed her trust in him ... even since the accident? Hadn't they sworn never to leave each other? In ten years of marriage, then since, he had never let her down - always been there. But if only she had managed to tell him ... about the baby.

The train stopped. They got out and walked along the platform ... towards the clock. . Jane pulled her coat around her and fastened the buttons with stiff, cold fingers. A harsh wind was blowing down from the hills, lifting her hair up and around and sending shivers down her spine.

'Alice... let's fasten your coat. It's cold.'

''t's all right, Mummy, I'm warm.' The child's hands were indeed warm against her mother's icy fingers.

'Hold my hand. Come here!' Jane was aware of her harsh voice. 'Keep away from the edge!'

Jane grasped her daughter's hand as they walked towards the huge station clock. The long hand swung into place - 11.59 - then 12.00. Suddenly, there he was, as if he had materialised from nowhere amidst the jostling passengers. She smiled. Just as handsome. Her heart leapt. He had not changed. But then ... would he ever? He smiled, showing perfect white teeth. His hair was as unruly as ever - with those same dark strands falling down around his forehead. He wore the same clothes: jeans, blue shirt, grey jacket - just as she remembered. She smiled back and forced herself to grasp the pale hand he held out; felt his touch melt into her own chilled hand. Why had she come?

They stood for a moment. She clasped Alice's still-warm fingers tightly, feeling, needing the reassurance of another human being.

'Mummy - you're hurting!''

'Sorry, darling.'

They walked towards the station cafe. She knew he would follow them to the usual table. He did, moving in perfect harmony, beside his child - the child he saw just once a year. Once seated, she ordered coffee. Toasted tea cakes. Alice's usual chocolate bun. The child tucked into her treats and sipped her milk quietly. Minutes passed but it felt to Jane as if they had climbed into a photograph - of life preserved forever, lovingly revisited, but in which time had ceased to exist.

The next train rumbled onto the platform outside. Noise! Scuffling! Travellers jostling to find their seats. He smiled at the child - studied her face - gazed longingly into her eyes. Then he looked at Jane with a strange, sad expression. He knew. They both knew - this was the last. Their time was over. Outside, on the platform, the whistle blew. The train left.

Then Jane was forced back to that fateful day ... hour ... minute ... split second - when life fell apart around her. That other train. Noise. People jostling forward. Pushing ... shoving. Stumbling! The fall! The ambulance! The blood! That eerie silence - as everything stopped!

'Come, Alice, we need to go.'

'But we haven't been anywhere!'

Nevertheless, the child stood obediently. Jane waited for him to make the first ... final move. A smile. He blew a kiss. A last goodbye - before floating, drifting upwards. His body faded slowly before her eyes, as if becoming enveloped by a thick smog. She shivered: watched him merge into the clock face - limbs losing definition ... features distorted - slowly, gradually, as if he couldn't bear to leave. Jane stared, mesmerised at the black, Roman numerals, her eyes clouded by tears - just as his eyes vanished. Nothing.

'Mummy, why are you staring at the clock? Is it those funny numbers?'

'Yes, love. They are funny, aren't they?'

'Mummy, why are you crying?'

'I'm just ... happy. Come on - let's go home.'

It was time for truth. Time to move on.

I AM THE LORD YOUR GOD: YOU SHALL NOT HAVE STRANGE GODS BEFORE ME

The Cult

ANNE WINNARD

It is a sultry humid evening; storm clouds huddle together. Thunder rumbles in the distance. Birds sing the mournful song that always seems to precede storms.

The trees are heavily laden with greens of various hues. Bare shaded patches of earth form irregular patterns among the verdant greens of the grass.

The darkness is eerie, ominous. Something is wrong. It feels like those dire moments of a nightmare just before one awakes.

The flowers of the forest droop, bending low as if to protect themselves from the oncoming storm.

Something scuttles past, reverses and runs over my feet. What is it? Not a rat, not a rabbit, not a fox nor a squirrel. It is furry, brown, black and grey with white circles around its enormous wide eyes. About the size of a small cat, it has a long bushy tail.

For a while, we stare at each other. I am too afraid to move and have the urge to scream. I fear the animal will pounce. But no! Twitching its whiskers, tail stiffened, it turns and smoothly darts away. Mesmerised, I follow.

The rain is now falling in large heavy blobs. I can barely see where I am heading. The chase leads me to a fast flowing river and the mystery animal slips away down the steep bank and disappears. I try to follow. The slope is far too slippery and dangerous.

I scramble back up the bank. As I stumble deeper into the forest, I spot a dim light somewhere in the distance. I walk towards the light and discover a singled story, flat-roofed building stretching way back into the trees. The building is made from natural stone.

I knock on the heavy panelled locked door. There is a key in the lock.

Thunder and lightning have always worried me and tonight's storm seems ultra-aggressive and violent.

I turn the key and enter. I find myself in a sparsely furnished room. The walls are decorated with large pictures of animals resembling the one I had pursued.

I open the door at the rear of the room. This door leads into another room furnished with parallel rows of approximately twenty bunk beds. As in the former room, the walls are adorned with pictures of the mystery animal.

Now I can hear chanting from yet one more room.

Cautiously, I lift the latch, open the door and slip unnoticed into the back of the room where I find some sort of ritual taking place.

I am really terrified. All participants are bare-footed and are wearing long, hooded, grey and white robes. All faces are covered with masks like the face of the unidentified animal.

The person closest to the door hands me a robe and a mask. I hastily put them on, removing my footwear.

The chanting continues. I notice a huge, gilt-framed picture on the front wall and am no longer surprised to see it is my animal again.

As the chanting stops, the congregation drop to the floor with heads bent as if in prayer.

I sneak a look to see what is going on. I am horrified. At the front there are three white tables. On each table lies the mystery animal pinned down as if to be dissected. In front of the tables stand three hooded figures. Each holds a scalpel above their head. I can hear just one voice from a higher level chanting some sort of orders to the three.

The three follow the order, making uniform patterns with their scalpels.

That is when I scream out.

The congregation turns. Hands try to grab me as I try to make my escape the way I came.

I am outside. I have no shoes and the storm is at its peak. Which way shall I run? Where am I? I am lost.

I hear them as they angrily hunt me down. There is no escape and I surrender.

Now, I am in a tiny room with no light, no window and a locked door. I still wear the bizarre uniform of the sect. I must await my fate.

REMEMBER THE SABBATH DAY TO KEEP IT HOLY

Sizzing Up

BILL CAMERON

As a kids on the street, we would 'sizz up' to make choices at the start of a game, for example which end of the slope had our goals; who would have first pick, who would be the cops and the robbers and so on. We waved our hands about to the refrain 'sizz-pap-brick' - street-patois 'scissors, paper brick (or rock).

The game is universal, but consider an apocryphal origin.

There were many secret signs to identify fellow Christians in the days of Roman persecution.

The Easter story could be signed with three fingers signifying the nails that pinned our Saviour to the cross; a fist the rock that sealed the tomb and a palm the shroud left in the tomb at the resurrection.

A circular sequence combined these metaphors into the game, with each sign overruling one and being trumped by the other.

The rock blunts the nails.

the nails tear the shroud

the shroud wraps the rock.

And the rock blunts the nails and so on...

The game could even be played in silence, recalling the somber sequence from Good Friday to Easter Sunday.

Friday (nails) - Saturday (rock) – Sunday (shroud).

Over time, the symbolism was secularized and scissors replaced the nails, the shroud became paper and rock became a brick, hence; scissors - paper – brick and 'sizz-pap-brick.'

So when children 'sizz up' they are recognizing and reiterating the Christian message of Easter Sunday.

YOU SHALL NOT COMMIT ADULTERY.

Simon says.

Lillian Hassall

Simon decked his cap to all the ladies, young, elderly and old . If it were raining, Simon would be there with his gentleman umberella to cover the delicate hairstyles and pretty hats of the wealthy females. He appeared to be a woman's dream.

But there was another side to Simon. He was a travelling man, going abroad to France, Italy, Spain. Travelling the width and breadth of England and of the world. What was he doing? Simon could be gone for weeks, maybe months. Maybe he's a spy? I'm his wife and I am rich. I call myself Judith that's all anyone needs to know. I've employed a private investigator to follow, no matter where or when, money is no object. I've picked an investigator who is slim, small and inconspicuous and he comes highly recommended. His name is Mr Roberts.

My beloved is home again the first of October. I've had instructions from Mr Roberts who knows how to follow, how to find. The first thing I will do is put a trace on his mobile, his computer and laptop. I've had an invite to visit Mr Roberts in his office. On the walls of his office, maps from all over the world all connected to his computer haven. He's committed, extremely expensive, but he will get the job done and it'll be worth every penny. I am so excited to have Simon home.

He arrived home on the evening of the first of October. Paula, our cook, our everything, cooked an amazing dinner, red wine and candles to decorate the dinner table. It had been a long journey. Simon was tired. A nice hot bath will help you relax and go to bed. In the morning you can tell me about your journey.

The next morning, we were up, showered and had breakfast.

'It's a beautiful morning. Want to take the dogs for a walk in the woods?'

He answered back, 'I'll just finish my breakfast then we can go. You get the dogs ready.'

I got Benny and Jackie ready - golden retrievers are a handful. They were our family.

Two weeks went by so fast. It was time for Simon to go on his travels.

'I'm not looking forward to you going again. It's been so lovely having you home.'

We hugged each other, Simon tried to console me, tears filled my eyes.

'I have to go - it's my job. Won't be long, then I'll be home again.'

'I know, it's just I love you very much and I miss you.'

'I'll have to get my bags ready.'

'Come on then, it'll keep me occupied.'

I know it might sound callous, two-faced, but I need to know. So it gave me the perfect chance to put the bleep in its hidden place. I drove Simon to the airport, after another hug, he got out and retrieved his bags. With a wave and a smile, he was gone.

I rang Mr. Roberts and told him that Simon had begun his journey to God knows where and that I had placed the bleep in his baggage.

'OK, my computer is on, I'll sync it with the maps and let you know later.'

It was three fifteen, Simon would be in the air.

Nine o'clock Mr. Roberts phoned. 'Your husband is in France; when he landed, he was met by a dark-haired lady with little ones, a boy and a girl. If it's OK with you, I'll get the next flight to France and follow the bleep.'

Mr. Roberts had been a private detective for years. In the old days today's technology didn't exist. Today there's more precision; he never got used to taking photos of people's private lives. This was the job, his business. He followed the bleep of Simon. It led Mr. Roberts to Mérignac Airport, and a house in Bordeaux.

The curtain moved and all at once the front door opened and stood in the door a blonde lady with three kids, one in arms. 'Hmm! Interesting' As Mr Roberts put his guilt aside and began to take pictures of the lady with her arms around Simon, and the children, except the babe in arms, were hanging round Simon's legs.

Mr. Roberts sent the photos plus a digital report. I viewed the photos and concentrated on reading the report. Feelings of hurt, anger, regret, confusion, more anger. I loved Simon so much, asking the same question over and over, how could he be so cruel? With tears streaming from my swollen eyes.

After a while I renewed contact with Mr. Roberts to ask him to keep doing the job and that's what Mr. Roberts did. He had this interesting task. His gut feeling was this man had a continuing story and Mr. Roberts would continue to stick to him like glue.

Two weeks had gone by. For Simon and this family, the time had come to say their goodbyes. Now where was Simon going next? Mr Roberts was ready to move. The bleep was on its way back to the airport. Simon wasn't going home he was on his way to Spain.

He knocked on a door in San Sebastián. A dark haired lady with two boys in tow answered the door. Big hugs all round. Déjà vu, Simon! Another two weeks. More photos to me. This was humiliating. I was confused even more, now I was very angry. I rang my solicitor Emma Hallward just to explain all that had gone on, showing photos and the reports. In the meantime another two weeks, another country, another family. Then leaving Europe for America, another family. More photos, more reports. Then back to England and home.

Four European countries, then America and back to me. This man Simon gets around. Emma Hallward had been investigating Simon.. Her report was brought back to Judith.. Simon was a polygamist having six marriages and so many children.

Such a busy man. Naturally there are six divorces to follow.

YOU SHALL NOT COVET YOUR NEIGHBOUR'S WIFE.

Lonely Hearts Column

AUDREY EDWARDS

Male, forty several, six foot, artistic, own house and car, good sense of humour, attentive, likes dancing and cooking WLTM similar for nights in or out.

Wow, likes cooking, what a catch, too good to be true do you think? I know from past experience, people's views of their attributes are greatly exaggerated.

On more than one occasion I have made a hasty retreat to my car, and escaped as quickly as possible. Leaving 'attentive attractive' without a backward glance.

As good as this one sounds on paper he is probably a pasty faced wimp from the shallow end of the gene pool, with a pimply back.

I think I'll give it a miss, stay in and have a curry, yeah!

YOU SHALL NOT KILL

Shane – The Final Shoot-out

BILL CAMERON

He thought he might have escaped his past by changing his name and taking work as a manual farm hand on the opposite edge of the state of Wyoming. But the rumour from Cheyenne was that a young stranger had turned up in Laramie out to prove himself against the gunslinger Charlie Grant. The surly Texan reflected on the number of times he had had to move on to avoid another reputation–hungry challenger. But all too frequently he had to leave town after killing another kid who had more bravado than his gun skills could support. Was he ever going to get a chance to settle without looking over his shoulder? A wry smile grew behind the matted grey beard and he reminisced on the last time he felt there was a chance to holster his six-shooter for good. Was it already ten years ago? But Marion had already been married to Joe Starrett - and Joe was as honest a guy as he'd ever met. And there was no chance a gunslinger, even with good intentions, was going to be a substitute father for eight-year-old Joey. There weren't many role models from the sparse settlements in the Grand Tetons of North West Wyoming so Shane, as he was then known, was idolised by the impressionable young Joey.

Standing up to boss Ryker and his thuggish trail boss Callaway was enough in its own right to make him a hero. When Shane belted on his gun to face up to a hired professional killer called Wilson, overawed Joey could hardly breathe. After leaving the murderer face down in the dust, the handsome stranger had to quit the sharecropper homestead with unfulfilled dreams of how life might have been with Marion and Joey. He

106

could have won them if he'd let Starrett face up to Wilson and death by the gun of the hired killer. Although Shane had led a violent life himself and had a name as a callous hard man, he had a fundamental ethic that respected and upheld the idea of family. He had, therefore, maintained an aloof distance from Marion. He left the Grand Tetons a with a nostalgic regret and haunted by the memory of Joey's plaintive plea, "Shane, Shane. Don't go." Subsequent events would suggest he ought to have remained to help Joey grow up.

At first he tried a life prospecting for silver further out west around Nevada. Known there as Jake Ransome, he eventually established himself as a cowhand but a quarrel in a bar over a game of poker resurrected his gun-fighting career and he buried one of Carson City's most important sons. Once more he had to pack and leave quickly. This pattern followed him through brief months in Deadwood; a couple of years in Denver and a mere few hours in Idaho Falls. He could not find peace, let alone a wife and family, anywhere in the expanding and unruly west

And now, after a decade, he was getting tired of running. Sporting a shaggy beard, sun-bleached hair and desert-weary grim face, he no longer walked so tall – many years of breaking horses and cattle had deformed his stature. Disfigured by an ugly purple scar, a souvenir of Tombstone where he almost lost an eye, he wouldn't now be recognised as the strong, slim and proud gunslinger shown on wanted posters of only a short while ago. This time, he told himself, he would back down and let his challenger take the glory and the mantle as the fastest gun.

He tracked down the youngster, boasting the handle of the Wyoming Kid, at a table in the Golden Wheel. The cowhand dealing stud pointed out Charlie Grant to the youngster. The Kid folded on what onlookers said looked like a winning hand. Maybe he felt that aces and eights would again prove the unlucky *dead man's hand* as it had been for Bill Hickok.   He sidled up to the bar and deliberately spilled Charlie's beer.

'Easy there, son,' he said to the youngster.

'I ain't no illegitimate son of yourn.   You calling my ma some kind of a tramp, mister?

'That ain't what I said youngster.   Just trying to avoid a set-to as you're a stranger in town and don't know me.   You want to be careful who you pick a fight with hereabouts.'

Imagining another notch on his gun, the youth turned, picked up Charlie's beer and poured it down his shirt.

Without a glance at his advisor, he sneered out of the corner of his mouth, 'Don't you talk down to me old man.   I think you and me got a noontime date on Main Street.'

Charlie knew where this was going and there was no way out. He had at least tried the pacifist approach.

'Noon then.' he said, turned and left the bar.

The old man went back to his room, shaved off his untidy beard, washed, ran a comb through his unruly hair and tidied himself up.   After cleaning his six-gun, he belted on his holster and went out into the desert to practise his quick draw.   Finding he had lost none of his speed gave him no satisfaction.

Old habits die hard.   He took to the street and pulled his hat low on his forehead to shade his face.   He made sure the sun would be behind him and so blaze into the kid's eyes when he left the Golden Wheel.   He stood, balanced and relaxed, waiting to teach another headstrong youth the error of his ways.

At noon they faced each other.   The kid couldn't see Charlie's face in the shadow of his black Stetson. The aging gunfighter waited for the first twitch that would tell that his adversary was making his move. He spotted the almost imperceptible tic in the kid's eyes and his hand went down to draw the colt 45.   In that split second, he recognised the pale blue eyes he had last looked into all those years ago – and realised they were so much like his mother's.

His hand froze on the weapon. He whispered the question, 'Joey?'

He could not draw the weapon from its holster - but the youngster did.

The force of the bullet smashing into his chest spun him round and sent his Stetson across to the sidewalk. He fell to the dusty sand in the street face up, his life ebbing away and his face revealed to the lad. As his blood pooled in the dust, the town folk looked on.

The grown-up boy knelt beside his one-time hero with tears in his eyes and a prayer on his lips:

'Shane, Shane. Don't go.'

The Dark Path

BARRY SEDDON

John Royston's climb to fame began at school. He needed no help. Blind genetic chance had dealt him victory. He always won the annual marathon. His epic poems, with subtle links to the classics, won school magazine trophies. He was a renaissance man in the perfectly proportioned body of a 17-year-old boy.

We hard-working grammar school boys hated him.

At university he gave up biology because it was "too much like plumbing," and settled on media studies, an apparent step down. But he knew what he was doing. He used his inevitable high-flying result as a passport to *The Times,* where he soon became its most provocative columnist, as much in front of the TV cameras as behind his desk.

Then one night his ego led him astray. During a TV discussion he proposed a theory that the only true way to write about something, however nasty, was to go out and do it. He was challenged and, sensing the mood going against him, he tempered the theory. Simply dreaming the experience would be enough, he said, for a hyper-intelligence such as his.

So he dreamed his way (he said) into the mind of a terrorist hijacking an airliner; of being a Kray twin; about climbing into Everest oblivion; about a jungle rumble with Cassius Clay. Not one of them actually featured in a dream of course, but his stories were brilliantly written, fuelling his endless need for fame.

Then he hit the slippery slope. He said that he had now learned how to dream his way into someone's dreams. That as Ian Brady, for instance, he had shared that terrible man's horrific dreams, then dreamed how Brady had felt when he was making them into nightmare reality.

It was meant to be a mental trick, another cynical headline-maker. But self-persuasion then led John Royston down a much darker path.

They caught him in the middle of slaughter number three. In the dock he smiled as he boasted about the genius of his technique. He was still smiling as he walked away, along the path of madness to a lifetime alone with his dreams.

YOU SHALT NOT BEAR FALSE WITNESS.

Where there's a Will...

ALAN RICK

'Glad you were persuaded to take it on?' Henry darted the question at his companion in the next seat. 'I think you will be when the goodies come rolling in,' he continued, gazing out of the window of the 'plane in which they travelled.

'I hope so,' replied Bert. Henry noted the expression in his face that showed that Bert's doubts were at last fading.

'Thank goodness,' he silently mused, 'don't want to be lumbered with a half-hearted partner-in-crime.'

The plane droned on – an albatross pressed into the service of the mass tourist market. They had boarded at Singapore bound for London two days after a report of the death of Sir Percival Lancer in London, had appeared in the press; his will would be read at the office of the family solicitor and any person with a seeming entitlement under the estate should attend at the reading. The conspiracy started almost instantly.

'Amazing how relations suddenly appear out of thin air when there's a will.' mused Henry enigmatically, 'Ask any solicitor - he'll tell you.'

'Suppose you're right,' answered Bert in his usual flat monotone.

'Too true I am – sometimes they haven't been seen for years – and sometimes ever,' added Henry, leaning forward with a glint in his eye that mingled amusement with malevolence; 'sometimes a relative appears who the others never even heard

112

of.' Henry paused to allow this seed to germinate in the mind of his accomplice. It fell upon stony ground.

'What are you on about?' asked his bewildered friend.

'What I am on about my old son is that such a relative should appear on this very occasion.'

'Eh!' ejaculated Bert with a start.

'A relative with acting ability.'

'With acting ability?'

'And of the right age group to the deceased.'

'Right age group?'

'And with a faint resemblance to Sir Percival.'

'Resemblance?'

'I have that man clearly in my vision even as we speak.'

'You have?' cried Bert with an unusually animated burst.

'I have!'

'Who is it then?' exclaimed an astonished Bert.

'You!' Henry thundered with a triumphant flourish.

It was following this conversation in a Singapore café that the two conspirators – for such they now were – put together the plan to produce a long lost and unheard of brother to Sir Percival. After all, the only person able to confirm that the deceased had no brother was the deceased himself and as Henry put it, 'dead people ain't known for being talkative.'

They had cooked an appetising dish but it was given added flavour by a crucial ingredient. The wife of the deceased had predeceased him by several years and they had had no children.

'All very neat and tidy,' chortled the intrepid Henry, 'It's very nice to see that when some leave this world they leave their affairs in an uncomplicated condition so they can be dealt with in an orderly manner. I spoke to the solicitors and they said you might find it interesting to witness the disposal of the estate,' he declared sipping his beer with a benignly complacent air.

Now the aircraft carried them on a fateful journey, one which mingled promise with danger in roughly equal measure, but just now it was the former that was uppermost in the minds of the two passengers. It had even begun to seriously dawn on the mind of the plodding Bert that a crock of gold lay beckoning to them at the end of the journey that was already several hours long and more than halfway to their destination.

Once inside the café in London Heathrow Airport, Henry declared that it was time for what he grandly described as a 'briefing conference.'

'Briefing Conference?' Bert dully intoned, 'but we ain't barristers.'

'Megaphore innit? I was speaking in the perpendicular.'

'Whassat then?' Bert blankly enquired.

'Not given to flights of fancy are you?' continued an exasperated Henry, rolling his eyes to the ceiling. 'No poetry in you.'

Henry then detailed the plan. 'Here is our passport to be produced at the reading as evidence of your identity and relationship to the deceased.'

Bert stared at it, his bovine expression slowly registering surprise. 'But it ain't mine – look it's got a different birth date and name and a picture of someone else in it.'

Henry leaned slowly across the table fixing the hapless Bert with a patronising stare.

'That is supposed to be the idea, brainstorm, the correct details fronted by a photo of your less than assuming fizzog would reduce our chances of success to less than zero.'

Bert suddenly brightened, 'you can't have less than zero Henry.'

'Never mind, Einstein, never mind,' said Henry raising his hand to his forehead and his eyes to the ceiling again as if looking for divine guidance. 'Just follow the instructions and for Gawd's sake don't start thinking because then you'd be dangerous.'

Henry studied the passport lovingly.

'A fine masterpiece of the forger's art,' he sighed wistfully. 'Just shows you what villains there are in our midst though don't it?' he added with a sorrowful look.

At last our two hopefuls stood before the huge oak front door of the firm of solicitors who had the stewardship of the affairs of the late Sir Percival. Their imposing credentials – stretching back, it seemed, to 1837 – declared themselves on a highly polished brass plate, Messrs. Booker, Wills and Booker.

In the main office they were greeted by the senior partner's secretary, Miss Tudball, a lady of severe demeanour and indestructible virtue, according to the young clerk in the office.

Yes, the firm had received their letter announcing their intended visit, and indeed the rest of the relatives of the deceased were already in Mr. Booker's office in a state of high expectation. The pair were led by her into the hallowed sanctuary of Mr. Booker himself. This was a room that could have sprung straight out of a Dickens novel. It was oak-panelled throughout and its book-lined shelves stretched across the whole of the wall behind the senior partner's desk. These shelves were ranged with leather bound volumes of frightening erudition and with titles that seemed to be designed to ensure that the lay populace would not understand their meaning and would effectively deter them from opening the books and attempting to read them. The cover of one book showed that someone had actually sat down and written a whole book about *First Century Roman Jurisprudence*! Quite how that would help the client who was in dispute with the authorities over his gas bill was a mystery. All the learned professions have their own exclusion language accessible only to the initiated and the law is no exception.

Mr. Booker rose from his desk and extended the hand of greeting. He was a man whom the Victorian era had forgotten to take with it when it ended. Impeccably courteous, black-coated like a large beetle, with a stiff wing collar and a seraphim smile that would melt a polar iceberg.

'Do come in won't you,' he oozed, 'We have delayed the meeting pending your arrival.'

'Very accommodating, to be sure,' returned Henry trying to match the smile. Henry thought this was the way you talked in the presence of the exalted.

'A long lost brother, eh,' said Mr. Booker, 'surely a delightful thrill for *all concerned*,' he beamed at the collection of relatives seated round the room. *All concerned* continued to sit in stone-faced silence. If there was a delightful thrill in this new development then it had clearly escaped their notice.

'Well now, to the matter in hand.' Mr. Booker had assumed a serious manner, no doubt reflecting the pivotal role assigned to him in all this. The faces and manner of *all concerned* became more animated at these words, their expressions smug and righteous, and rightly so, for had they not all been kind and caring towards the deceased during his lifetime? Of course they had and is it not only proper that the deserving should be rewarded?

Mr. Booker opened the large envelope, took out the Will and began to read. The faces round him became visibly more concerned whilst trying not to appear so in the manner of the genteel. But what was this? A dark frown engulfed the face of the solicitor as he looked up.

'I must confess to being somewhat troubled' he said absently, 'I should have thought that if Sir Percival had had a brother then the fact would have emerged from the contents of the Will, but it is nowhere mentioned.'

It was fascinating to see the facial expressions among the ranks of *the concerned*. A moment before, they had registered nervous apprehension, but now they glowed with a coarse kind of satisfaction – perhaps the righteous would inherit the earth after all!

'Allow me to elucidate!' declaimed Henry in designer law-speak, 'this man,' pointing to Bert with all the dramatic gesture of a QC in full flow, 'this man is a fraud and an imposter!'

Mr. Booker blinked like a startled owl and the faces of *the concerned* struggled to decide which would be the appropriate expression to adopt – horror or delight. Bert, meanwhile, froze in his seat and took on the appearance of a man upon whom a tree has fallen.

'Perhaps I should introduce myself,' said Henry superfluously. 'Ex-Detective Sergeant Henry Watkins, now retired,' producing his card from an inside pocket and passing it across the desk to the slowly recovering solicitors.

'Why bless my soul, a most unfortunate occurrence to be sure, murmured Mr. Booker sorrowfully.

'Quite so,' said Henry, 'The man you see before you,' indicating the fast-disintegrating Bert, 'is not the man he has represented himself to be – he is, in fact, Albert Dodgson a criminal with a long record of petty offences and several prison sentences to his credit.' Henry then regaled the assembly with a detailed account of how he had met Albert in Singapore, inveigled him into playing the part of the long-lost brother, organised false identity documents for him and brought him to London, ostensibly to claim his inheritance.

'A little personal project of mine,' murmured Henry, 'I was the only one in the station who had never managed to nick – er – apprehend him and I wanted to put that right as a little recreation for my retirement.'

'Dear me,' sighed Mr Booker, 'I fear that this little affair will not go down well at the Law Society – a question of our firm's good name, don't you know.'

The concerned had become visibly more upright in their seats, backs straighter than ever – were these halos that seemed to have formed above their heads? Or just imagination perhaps?

Later in the saloon bar opposite the office, Henry enjoyed a well-earned pint with his former colleague, detective sergeant Sam Oliver and took mental stock.

'I seem to be the only winner in this matter – Albert doing time again, but this time on my account,' he reflected as he finished his drink. Suddenly he exploded in laughter, 'Them relatives, what a crew – their faces!' he spluttered to his companion. 'You should have seen them when the solicitor finished reading and then I realised what they meant by an 'interesting disposal of the estate' Old Perce had left his entire estate to the Ornithological Bird Sanctuary with a special request to use the money to research into the migratory habits of the lesser duck-billed platypus!'

Sam Oliver chuckled, 'Especially interesting to Bert facing a period doing bird himself.'

'Oh well,' said Henry easing himself off the bar stool, 'they may not have got what they wanted but I certainly did.'

Henry went out into the busy street whistling, a spring in his step, with the air of a man at peace with himself at last.

Three Clues

Although very quickly on the scene of the dead man at his home;

Alerted by his visiting mother who had dialled 999 from her 'phone

CID officers were baffled as to what did it all mean - yet wonder

Because there were clues a-plenty around upon which to ponder

For amongst scattered items on the living room floor

Lying near the corpse was a domino – the double four.

Also close by from an 80-piece box was a jigsaw piece

Such clues an intrigued Press would wish to quickly release

Particularly of knitting needles pointing to a photo of a bride

119

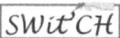

The murderers – disturbed by Ma – thought he had died

But the corpse with his last breath had tried to reveal

His killers, before he slumped over on a rug of chenille

A young fluffed-faced policeman suddenly raised a finger

No need in his eyes any more to conjecture or linger

A 4 x 4 estate truck parked under a nearby tree

Had been reported having a number plate JIG 80C

Registered in the name of the wife's supposed lover

As intimated by the corpse's hysterically sobbing mother

She had unexpectedly dropped by because of the strife

Her son had been through due to his untrue wife

But where were these presumed killers – had they fled?

No – they were found hiding under the matrimonial bed!

ROSEMARY SWIFT

120

HONOUR YOUR FATHER AND YOUR MOTHER.

Where is Amethyst?

BILL CAMERON

The smell of *Peach Pie*, the drug-driven rock band, told me that I was closing in on this latest commission. A nauseating cocktail of sweat, alcohol, tobacco and cannabis assaulted my nostrils as I slipped behind the stage amongst the road crew, technicians and hangers-on. And the noise from the stage hardly qualified as music or entertainment.

'Not the most pleasant job, I've ever had,' I thought, 'I'll be glad when it's over and I can get back to following wayward husbands and investigating insurance scams.'

The assignment had at first seemed impossible, but you don't turn down a gang boss like Eddie Moscetti without comparing your possible future against the probable absence of one. Very few people found they could refuse a Moscetti offer. Eddie 'Scarface' Moscetti hadn't exactly requested my one-man agency to find his headstrong daughter, but I knew he had a job that would demand my investigative energies twenty-four seven. Moscetti knew I was good at my job and would deliver on demand, even though we frequently operated on opposite sides of the law.

I was feeling happier now that I was nearing the end of the search for the recalcitrant teenager.

The quest had started three weeks ago and Moscetti was getting impatient. I had done well from the initial brief information I had been given. Chantreuse, the fifteen-year-old, had disappeared after another confrontation with her father over any one of a zillion teenage peccadillos that irritated the gangster, who liked his wickedness up front and full-on. I looked at her photograph again: very pretty, but too much make-up for one so young – why can't they accept the beauty of puberty without trying to grow up so quickly? I remembered how Moscetti had told me that she had mentioned hanging out at Peach Pie concerts and had heard her on the phone to a new friend called Amethyst. With a name like that, I figured, she was probably another spoilt rich kid with more of Daddy's money than was good for her and a lifestyle aspiration fashioned on her glamour model mother. Probably public school educated with little or no parental influence – in fact, a copy of Chantreuse Moscetti. A heavy metal band like Peach Pie would have its attractions for a pair of teenagers, wrestling with puberty and its aftermath. It seems the friendship had started at a concert in Berlin last summer, during a school trip from the Paris academy that cost a small fortune in protection racket proceeds.

The innocent girls must have been seduced by the noise, drugs and alcohol culture that attracted a following of spotty boys, impressionable girls and long-haired goths of indeterminate gender – or none. I had been no more than a day or two behind the band at each venue in their European Millennium MegaBlast tour but had not yet made contact. Interviews with the occasional straggling fan kept me up to date with the extremely unsociable behaviour of the hedonistic band and their arrogant treatment of young girls especially. The stories I heard made me more determined to fulfil my employer's wishes. I might not like his business but at least he didn't exploit young girls.

And here I was now in a dingy night club in Leeds, passing myself off as a booking agent to get backstage where I could get a good look over the throbbing dancefloor. Somewhere amongst this screaming, sweating, head-banging hoard were Chantreuse and her friend Amethyst. I needed to locate and remove them with as little fuss as possible. But I did not fool myself to expect a peaceful rescue of the pair who would be under the influence of teenage hormones and music-fuelled adrenalin. I desperately hoped that such natural chemistry would not have been enhanced by any other vile substance that circulates events like this.

I stepped into the wings and looked out. The stage was three quarters full with the massive drum kit; the remainder cluttered with amplifiers and vibrating speakers. A slim corridor over the footlights was where three sweating rock guitarists postured, paraded and screamed into the microphones. The band was notorious for extreme stage stunts, using explosions, smoke, fire and foam cannons to hide their musical shortfall. Now, the lead singer was doing his Mexican stunt, swigging from a bottle of tequila and eating raw, and allegedly very hot, chilies. Personally I prefer the taste of chicken to chili.

Looking over the crowd I decided that I wasn't going to pick out my quarry in the dark from the packed swaying mass of sweating flesh. I left the club and took a seat by the window in the bar across the road. I would question the road crew later. I had heard the name Amethyst mentioned in smatterings of conversations between some of the groupies, so I guessed that she was a regular and they would be able to point her out. She could then lead me to the disobedient daughter.

I knew the gig had finished when punters started to fill the bar. The band was booked for three nights at this club so the road crew did not need to hang around long after the band finished its encore. I recognised the leather-jacketed, tattooed and pierced-nose archetype roadies as three of them entered the bar.

'That'll save me a walk,' I told myself and got to the bar as the first of the roadies swaggered up.

'What can I get you lads?' I offered.

An eighteen stone gorilla looked down at me, 'We usually kick off with a double Jack Daniels and Coke after a hard night's work. But as you're paying, you'd better get the bottle and two cans of Coke. Then we'll decide if we're going to get you what you want. It's not autographs, is it?' he smiled, presenting an array of black teeth, gold fillings and gaps.

'Can't beat straight talking,' I conceded, 'I'm looking for a couple you might know, called Amethyst and Chantreuse.'

The gorilla smiled again and so did his pals. 'Try the Astoria Motel. They're booked into the honeymoon suite.' The road crew laughed out loud.

I finished my beer and thought about what Moscetti would do when he found out that his precious child's relationship was neither platonic nor orthodox. But that would be a problem for Chartreuse; all I had to do was to find the child and bring her home. I muttered a thank you to the roadies, dropped another few notes on the table and left for the Astoria. I could still hear them laughing as I walked out into the street with the valediction, 'Look out for Amethyst,' ringing in my ears.

The desk clerk at the motel was co-operative after a couple of notes crossed the table and it was easy to locate the so-called honeymoon suite. From the passage I couldn't see what made this different from the other rooms, but experience told me that this would be the room with the selection of toys and special videos - and the hidden cameras.

I knocked at the door gently, got no answer, then a little louder.

A gruff voice, clearly from London's East End, minced no niceties in telling me to go away, but I had come too far to be repelled by strong language - my search was reaching a conclusion.

'I'm looking for my friend Chantreuse,' I called.

The door swung open. A six foot four, eighteen stone heavy metal drummer, bald, bearded and tattooed, cut out the light from inside the small room.

I put on a smile, 'I'm a fan of Peach Pie, same as her and I've come to take her back home to Daddy. Is Amethyst in there as well, please?'

'You don't know nuffin' about Peach Pie and rock music do yer? I am 'Ammer Fist, stupid. Get my name right yeh! Do you wanna know why I'm called 'Ammer Fist?'

I thought back to the roadies' parting caution and then I realised what they meant when they said, "Look out for Amethyst." Hammer's clubbed fist sent me hurtling across the hotel corridor with one crunching blow. The hotel door slammed as I slammed into the opposite wall. A few minutes were all I needed to get my breath back. I've had conflicts with harder hitters than this moron and he was going to wish he had been more co-operative.

I downloaded a Peach Pie track to my phone and placed it on the floor outside his door, volume wound up to max. Standing at the side of the door I knocked rapidly and waited. The door swung wide and the drummer stepped out. He stopped in his tracks, puzzlement written all over his ugly face, mouth agape as he spotted my phone. The fire extinguisher glanced off his temple and smashed his shoulder blade, in billiards parlance a perfect cannon. He slumped to the deck, face down and dazed to the deck as the nausea from the busted scapula hit his stomach. I pinned him to the floor and whipped out an industrial cable tie, a multi-use aid which I always carry, and strapped his two pinkies together. No matter how big they come, very few men have the strength or can apply sufficient leverage to separate bonded little fingers. He was going nowhere for some time. I looked into the room. I recognised the tearful child on the bed from her photograph. No make-up now, rivers of tears running through purple, orange and blue blotches. Patterns repeated on her bare arms and legs.

'Chanteuse,' I said, 'Your Daddy sent me to bring you home. You should call me Uncle Jim and I'm here to look after you. Would you like to clean yourself up, then get your coat and we can go?'

'OK,' she whimpered, 'I hope Daddy will still love me after what I've done.'

'Don't you worry,' I tried to reassure her, 'He never stopped loving you. I'll wait in the corridor.'

Outside, a pathetic Hammer Fist was sitting in a pool of vomit, moaning and feeling very sorry for himself. I considered inflicting more pain on the despicable scum, or even calling Scarface, who would without doubt arrange to terminate the pervert's career behind the drums – he deserved no better. Instead, I called it in to the police. So long as I kept on the right side of the law, I might not get offered any more commissions from the likes of Moscetti.

After stepping over 18-stone of what was left of a tough guy, accidentally stamping on his outstretched knee, I looked down on the pained grimace, 'Yeh, mate. Now I've got your name right – paedophile! And the world is going to know it as well!'

I took Chantreuse home to Daddy the same evening, hiring an executive limo on Daddy's account. I didn't wait to give him the full story. I left with, 'I'll send my bill in the next couple of days, but please no more work and I don't need our endorsements among your associates, thank you very much.'

126

Tapestry of Time

BARRY SEDDON

Her fingers hurt. They pulsed with the need to bleed. But Jenny dared not bleed and therefore, around the base of each finger, she had bound lengths of wool that had failed the test of brightness. Her friends were also finger-bound as they pushed and pulled their yarn-freighted needles. Jenny's back ached as she crouched over the dimly-lit tapestry, the work that was long in time and longer still from end to end.

Moll, her dearest friend, once told her that their shining task, though made here in the land of their birth, would one day be taken across the sea to a great city called Bayeux in the land from whence came William, their new sovereign, the conqueror who had slaughtered their heroic King Harold.

Now, at William's behest, under the saintly eye of Canterbury's Archbishop, Jenny and Moll and the scores of needlewomen who worked with them on the great tapestry toiled for hours each day and often into the twilight. The great and beautiful work grew slowly, its pictures of battles and fabled animals and noble lords telling the story of a once-great land, subdued by an invader.

Sometimes, slowly standing straight at the end of a long and weary day, Jenny would see her work in all its glory, a band of sturdy linen as far across as her arm could reach, threaded with the history of her land. And she would smile with pride, and go to her bed, picturing the work when it was complete. Some said that when it was done, perhaps after ten more years, its length would measure 70 man-strides, though she could not credit this as true.

Before she slept, Jen sometimes wondered if her talent would be wasted. Would it fall to dust like her body and blow away? Or would it somehow ride the wind for years until, one day, a baby girl, gasping her first breath, took in that dusty talent? Might it then grow and cause the child to turn to the beauty of thread and cloth and art, and pass on her skill to others? And in that distant time, might that baby, that young girl, that woman, live in Jenny's own land? Might she even travel to William's land across the sea and admire Jenny's work, perhaps in the cathedral of ancient Bayeux?

For Meg

In dreams, it hangs upon the air,

her lovely voice, but no-one's there.

It echoes in my lonely head

and whispers softly, "Come to bed."

Her smoky voice drifts down the wire

as I stand, pensive, by the fire.

The warmth I feel is not from coals

but from the years when two young souls

believed that life could bring no pain.

In dreams it hangs, again, again

BARRY SEDDON

128

After Military Service

ANNE WINNARD

Joseph Daniel O'Brien, commonly known as Joe, described his life as boring and monotonous. He had been dismissed from the army after his time in Afghanistan. He suffered from post-traumatic stress, difficult to diagnose, and even more difficult to treat.

Most days he stayed in bed until pub opening time at midday. He kept within his budget making sure he could cover his utility bills and rent. He didn't have a washing machine, but then he didn't need one. Two pairs of jeans and two Manchester City tee shirts were his uniform.

Personal cleanliness was not high on Joe's list. People would frequently move away from him. BO mixed with tobacco was not a pleasant aroma.

Once Joe was strong, but little action and much beer had given him a pot belly. He was short in stature, with a long, grey unkempt beard. Possibly livestock lived in it.

His short stubby fingers were nicotine-stained; his nails bitten down to the quick.

Joe had a pleasant temperament, usually so laid back he was almost supine, but over-indulgence in alcohol occasionally changed him into a black-hearted devil.

Things began to change one morning when he awoke in the local nick. Too much alcohol and one unpleasant remark had caused him to fly into an uncontrollable rage. He was arrested for his own safety and the safety of others around him, charged with attempted bodily harm and a breach of the peace.

Home again, he caught sight of himself. Ashamed at how far he had fallen, he showered, shaved, stripped his bed and set off to see his mother. Together they cried. She knew her son was returning to the Joe she knew. A job as an assistant in a local supermarket paid only minimum wage, but it was a start.

Afternoon boozing stopped. His tobacco habit was drastically reduced. He still enjoyed a pint on his day off, but in moderation. His days had order and his life had purpose.

His appearance changed too. He lost weight and his interest in photography returned.

One day he set off to photograph a well-known beauty spot, meaning to enter a competition. He climbed a tree for a better view, but crashed into a river when a branch snapped. He crawled up the bank over stones and mud, with unbearable pain down one side.

His car was parked some fifty yards away. It seemed an eternity before he reached the car park. Only one other car stood there, engine revving and ready to go. Joe shouted as loud as he could. Maybe he even screamed. But then he lost consciousness.

Liverpool to Manchester 1830

The fifteenth of September 1830, an historical event occurred, one of the opening chapters to the glorious age of steam.

Such a collection of technology had never before been seen.

Black shiny coal, superheated steam, painted iron and parallel rails to show the way.

Steam engines Rocket and Northumbrian will try to win this day.

The coming together of these mighty elements, forged together to form a team.

Stephenson and Locke together weld a dream.

Feted dignitaries and the captains of industry, transport power rarely seen.

The future in the hands of the men who care to dream.

Transport never dreamed of, goods and passengers to effortlessly convey.

Liverpool to Manchester- two hours and no delay.

Among the celebrations to mark a momentous start, a missed foot, a slippery hand, a loud pitiful scream. A tragedy marred this exciting day.

A gentleman Parliamentarian under the wheels did fall William Huskisson's name will forever leave its mark - transported to Eccles but sadly passed away.

No indication of the dangers had there been in undertaking such a momentous scheme.

Passenger safety and comfort had never been the theme.

This adventurous endeavour the whole world to display,

Their legacy around the world can still be seen today.

JOHN HASSALL

Destitute

Lillian Hassall

Once I was a baby, I had a mother and a father

I had a home, warmth, love and care,

I had a sister and a brother

I began to crawl, walk, run and climb

My life was humble, but we had food, clothes,

Then, over time,

People became angry, apathetic, and families fought

Aromas of burning, men with helmets on doing what they ought

No children playing, sadness filled the smoky air

Food was scarce, no clean water to drink,

Step out in the dark, we wouldn't dare

Father and mother gone, maybe dead, I do not know

I am alone, discarded, abandoned to my foe.

Our home is flattened to the brick filled ground. Where is my dog, my cat? It's deathly quiet, not a sound. I'm lying on an old cardboard box, shivering. My head is filled with memories, they're so confusing. What has happened to my family? I looked but nowhere to be seen. A nightmare, then my mind changes and I'm at home again. I want to sleep, but it's so hard to. Then I'm crying and then, I drift into sleep.

A voice enters my shattering mind,

'Little girl, do you want something to eat?'

My eyes open wide and see a man standing over me, it's getting dark. As my eyes adjust, as I ask him. 'Who are you?'

'My name is Mark.'

There is just a glimmer from the street light. He brushes the soot and dust from my face.

'I had a brother called Mark. He is gone with my sister and mother and father. They're gone to another place.'

'What is your name?'

'My name is Sally'"

Mark takes me by the hands and pulls me out of the rubble.

'Where are you taking me?'

'I'm taking you to see someone very special; they've been wondering where you are. They have worried, convinced you've got into trouble.'

He takes me down some old dusty steps, then around some windy corners. There's a small orange light in the distance. I can hear whispering voices, it feels warmer. Then people sat around a small fire, they look and stare at me. Then I can hear someone calling my name.

'Sally, oh Sally. Mark you've found Sally.'

Tears of joy, as my father, my mother and my sister throw their arms round myself and Mark. I cry, they cry. I ask my family

'What has happened? Where's our home? Why?'

'A big bomb exploded and our street fell. We've to stay here for safety, when they're ready they will ring a bell.'

We didn't know then but the war was to last another six years. Our home had been bludgeoned, we had strength together and yet there were fears. Fears of what to do next. People were angry, but then, they began to pull together. We all did.

Cleaning ourselves up as best we could, sister May, Mark, Father and my Mother. The kindness of other people, shone through like a sparkling penny.

Dad and Mark were conscripted into the army. Mother, May and myself got work in an ammunition factory. Dad and Mark may be home soon to join the family

The sun will shine again; peace will rain down on us. Keep smiling through the storm of guns,

'One day at a time' mother would say and caress May, Mark and Dad, all in a bundle close to her breast

Where No Birds Sing

Stinking of shit, they stand strong in ankle-high mud,
In trenches, leaning against rotting wood, rusty metal.
Stare, unseeing, across that charred and blackened place,
A land once blessed with colour and nature's bounty,
Before men had made it a space of still silence,
Bleached greyness, trees stripped of seasons, where no birds
sing.

They wait!

Dinner at eight! In the officers' dug-out, wine,
In fine, cut glass goblets - each hand raised to a toast.
Soup made with water, and little else. 'Pass the pepper.'
Cutlets, of something. Nobody asks. Three apricots,
Out of a tin, scraped up with spoons, from metal plates.

136

They wait!

Their men eat up top, hunched on a bench, dunk dry bread,
In weak tea, laugh, talk of home - as smiles mask their fear.
At this last supper, men with nothing in common,
But hope, pen letters to loved ones so far away.

And wait!

The shells drop with an ear-splitting boom! Smoke! Choking!
Silence! All breaths extinguished. Neither stench, nor mud,
Nor rain, nor sun will bother them. Their time has come.

But wait!

Their journey's end? Listen! Wind gently whispers, hums,
A hymn - accompanying souls to eternity.

They're gone.

Nothing moves. Naked waste - lifeless as the moon, where,

No birds sing.

SYLVIA EDWARDS

REPRINTED FROM ALAN RICK'S MEMOIRS; 'MY LIFE AND OTHER MISADVENTURES ISBN 978-1-326-60665-7

The Unmartial Spirit

ALAN RICK

My own angst-ridden adolescence had its share of farce and my two years of unmartial National Service in the Army were no exception – a lengthy exercise in human futility in an attempt to turn me into a soldier. On being posted to Egypt I remember thinking how unwise the government was to entrust the Suez Canal into my hands.

It was a dark cold day in January when I reported to Aldershot for the initial fourteen weeks training. It seemed to me like the unfolding of a nightmare, the tramp of boots, the barking of orders, the general air of profanity and the sight of grown men snapping to attention with a funny little salute. This was a culture shock to a young man who had never heard a swear word uttered in his own family circle.

We all reported to be "kitted out" which meant that, within the space of an hour, each one of us was weighed down with blankets, boots, webbing, mess tins, uniform and a .303 rifle. I could not believe this was actually happening to me and would have jumped into a hole had I been able to find one big enough.

We had to undergo a process called *documentation*. This consisted of filling up a form – a kind of resume of my entire life to date and which would end up on the regimental sergeant major's desk. I was intrigued by the section requiring me to state my occupation prior to call up. This was a problem as I had not had one – I was expecting to read for a university degree when the army rudely interrupted the process. I beckoned to the duty corporal and told him I could not fill in this section as it did not apply. He was aghast. He eyed me as if I was a dangerous subversive element.

"You must enter an occupation." he barked.

"But I can't do that because I've never had one," I countered plaintively.

His face registered panic and hostility in equal measure.

"This is Army form 496," he roared "You can't leave blanks – it has to be filled up."

"But what with? I've never had a job."

"Well just put anything down," he sighed.

Suddenly inspiration struck. Slowly and deliberately against the word *occupation* I entered *gentleman.* Later that day I was to learn the first golden rule – never try to be funny in the Army – you cannot win.

In due course the door of the billet burst open and in came the RSM – six feet tall, constructed like a stone building and with a voice that could blow a hole in a wall. He had my form in his hands and did not seem a happy man. He required to know – in a tone that made it clear that his enquiry was not a multiple choice question,

"Which one of you is S/22624917 Rick?"

"It is I." I gamely volunteered.

He fixed me with a stare. He was clearly not impressed with what he saw and intoned in a voice of mock irony;

"We appear to 'ave a member of the more exalted echelons in our midst."

My explanation fell on deaf ears.

"I do 'ope you will forgive me," he continued, his eyes gleaming with menace "but you see I 'appen to suffer from an unfortunate ailment – I've no sense of humour," he roared straight into my ear.

Later that night in the cookhouse and about five hundred peeled potatoes later, he visited me on his rounds. Apologising for not being able to provide me with an occupation "…more commensurate with your station in life," I was ordered me to get the whole sack of potatoes peeled by breakfast. Just an incident in my youth, but what a voyage of discovery!

Robert Blincoe

Whilst Wilberforce did rightly fight against slavery abroad,

The plight of children in English mills was sadly quite ignored.

One was a London seven-year old; Robert Blincoe was his name.

The tale of his painful childhood would later bring him fame.

Taken from St. Pancras Workhouse that for this waif was home.

Trundled days in a cart to Nottingham, his fate not sealed alone.

Parishes indentured their charges, until reaching age twenty-one,

Lure of good food and being schooled to northern mills they'd gone.

Instead these foundlings were misled, small hands and puny stature,

Used to deftly mend low threads so spinners could manufacture.

Constant toil in cotton fluff, fed on black bread and measly gruel.

Small limbs crushed or starved lives lost meant little to Masters cruel,

Other orphans took their place, no parents to mourn their passing.

No-one saw the oft change of face unless when inflicting a lashing.

Despite cheap labour this mill did fail, Blincoe to Derbyshire went.

One hundred to a dormitory, three to a bed, nights were spent.

Cruel overlookers playing games screwed vices on tender young ears,

Dangled over clunking looms despite their pleas and tears,

Blincoe's legs grew crooked; his body a weeping sore.

Ears badly scarred from torture; came the day he could take no more.

He ran to report a whipping; local magistrates curbed such abuse.

The malevolent-souled Mill owner had ignored such cruel ill-use.

This bully was not cowed by his equals nor affected by a Reform Act.

His water mill was to fail as steam-power was becoming the fact.

Blincoe upon reaching manhood, was a skilled stock-weaver,

Set up at home, wed Martha, he certainly was an achiever.

Alas, Blincoe's spinning wheel set on fire; for debt to prison was fated.

After this bad spell, his life went well; his three offspring educated.

In his Memoirs, of his children, Blincoe in anger retorted,

Rather than toil in a Mill, he'd have them all transported

ROSEMARY SWIFT

All Aboard

BARRY SEDDON

A gloomy November Sunday was closing in on a drab, damp and dreary midnight. My companion and I had often travelled this route at this time because, for reasons that might or might not become clear, it suited our purpose.

A near-empty train, I must say, is a restful way to travel. Although it stopped at 11 stations between Manchester Victoria and Wigan Wallgate, rarely more than four passengers would come aboard. Sometimes it hardly seemed worth running the train.

This journey was different from the start. My friend and I were the only ones on board the 23:20 from Victoria, but at the last moment, a poorly-dressed young woman tumbled aboard, breathless, tearful, and pushing a shabby trolley in which a baby was crying. She turned and headed further up the train, but not before I noticed that she had a black eye. She was about nineteen.

In the window seat, my friend S puffed contentedly on his Meerschaum pipe as I watched for the next stop, making a mental list. Anything to relieve the boredom. Here is what happened.

23.23. Salford Central. A small man joined the train. The cold had no obvious effect on him. He chewed on a short black pipe and was dressed like a music hall cartoon character. He also headed up the train, rolling with its motion with practised ease. I turned to say something to S but he simply raised a nonchalant eyebrow and went back to reading his newspaper.

I should mention here that my friend often travelled as a letter of the alphabet; just one of his many foibles. Inscrutable but endearing. He livened my life.

23.26. Salford Crescent. Three students, slightly merry, joshed and joked as they boarded and, once again, headed away up the train. Perhaps my friend's rather pungent pipe smoke was putting people off! Anyway, apart from the unusual number of passengers, things now seemed to have reverted to the humdrum.

23.33. Swinton Station Road. One workman in oil-stained overalls.

23.35 Swinton Moorside. Gent in his 50s, silver hair, silver-topped cane, dark evening dress shiny at the knees, carrying a little brown case with "Mr Marvel" embossed on the side in peeling gold leaf. Maybe a down-on-his-luck pub entertainer.

23.38 Walkden. Dewy-eyed young couple, gazing fondly at each other as they hip-bumped and giggled away from us.

23.42. Atherton. The overall man got off and trudged away. At this point, our journey began to be interesting again.

23.47. Hag Fold. Even S put down his newspaper and leaned back, nodding slightly as a sullen young man joined us. Extravagant sideburns, slightly greasy hair, black leather jacket with silver studs, knee-length boots, black eye makeup and ear pendants in the shape of silver skulls.

23.50. Daisy Hill. Three nuns, heads down, hands clasped together, murmuring to each other as they glided away.

23.54. Hindley. Clearly a lady of the night, looking, if you will pardon the expression, very much the worse for wear - and I do not mean inebriated. But despite her untidy bleached hair and much-too-high silver shoes, one with a broken strap, the clasp-bag she was carrying seemed to be very full and she was wearing a satisfied little smirk.

23.57. Ince. Two demure maiden ladies with a long-fringed sheepdog padding along with a resigned look under their unending stream of gossip.

Wigan Wallgate. Four minutes past midnight.   Terminus. Up we stood, out we stepped and silently we watched as our travelling companions walked away. Not separate or in silence, but chattering, laughing, arms around shoulders, mixing and mingling.

One nun cuddled up to the leather-clad youth, another Sister was giggling with the hussy and one student had paired up with the girl of the loving couple, whose erstwhile companion was leading the sheepdog. The shabby magician was carrying the baby, while tickling it under its chin. The girl with the black eye was pushing the empty trolley and sharing a joke with the students and the no-longer demure maiden ladies.

As they trooped away and Sunday retook the station, I turned, a question on my lips, but S forestalled me in his usual style, finger to his lips.

"My dear friend, there is no mystery. If only you would read the newspapers! Wigan is hosting a theatre festival. From what I have read, a director with ideas above his station had the idea of dispatching his cast to spend a week or two in the areas where their characters might have lived, wearing the right clothes at all times. Holds himself in high regard, according to today's *Times*.

"Anyway, the play opens tomorrow night. Fortunately, I have important business with my brother. He's up here on some secret civil service jaunt. You would probably be awfully bored, so I shall leave you to enjoy the play.

"You might even be able to wangle an invitation to the pre-show party. It's tomorrow afternoon. That's obviously what they are all heading for and therefore why they're all on the same train at this benighted hour.

"Sometimes I worry about you, but there is a remedy of course. You really must start reading *The Times*, my dear Watson."

Insomnia

AUDREY EDWARDS

It's 3 am. I can't sleep. I can taste the hot chocolate I had at midnight in the vain hope it would aid my insomnia.

The half-light afforded by the street lamp only serves to remind me I should be asleep. I can't understand why I don't drop off.

I said as much to my friend Shirl, yesterday: '300 thread count Egyptian cotton sheets, a £100 down duvet, a Tempur mattress.'

I regretted saying: 'What the blue buggering heck does it take to get a night's sleep?' I caught the look on her face - she doesn't like profanities. I, on the other hand, love them when it suits.

Oh, no, it's raining now. I'll never get off to sleep – the drip, drip, drip of the rain on the chimney cowl drives me crackers.

I wonder what Maeve Binchy would do? Probably get up, make a cuppa and write something really amazing.

My Land

My land brings me pride and my land brings me shame,
But both give me reason to shout out her name.
The pride comes from watching our tall cities grow,
The shame from the skulls and the bones down below.

For this land was built upon cruelty and greed,
When rich men bought servants to slave in their fields.
Ships brought them in thousands from distant dark shores
Whole families dying, piled under the boards.

And still now for thousands the misery goes on,
In splintered shack townships they starve in the sun.
So how, you might ask, dare I stand here so proud,
Shouting the name of my homeland so loud?

It has to be shouted, the world must be told,
How one seed brought evil that thrived upon gold
But one shining seed kept our slave folk alive
Their joy in the music that helped them survive.

For slaves brought us samba, their dances, their songs,
Salute that wild music, those drums and those gongs,
Let them echo through Rio, Brazil and the world,
And let us salute as hope's banner unfurls

We have to remember, we cannot forget
Those dark nights of agony, lingering yet
Long debts must be paid that have grown for an age
Let us give something back, let us turn back the page

BARRY SEDDON

Bus(es)

BARRY SEDDON

Rain will always fall to keep the world alive and sometimes it can ease a troubled mind. Gaze along a drizzle-misted city street at the dusky end of a weary day. Surely there is more to life than this! But then here comes a bus. Look more closely and imagine... It's not a single grey-brown monster looming from the mist but two soft shapes, the cheerful orange of one mirrored in the fresh-washed tarmac.

Two orange buses, dreaming through the double-dazzled brightness of the city, where a hundred neon lights are now two hundred and buses are magic summer charabancs, heading west to sun and sand and remembered smiles.

Rocket and its Engineers

LILLIAN HASSALL

Robert Stephenson was born to George Stephenson and Frances nee Sanderson on the 16th October 1803 at Willington Quay in Northumberland England.

Initially he attended a village school less than 2 miles from the family home, Long Benton.

When Robert was 11 years old his father sent him to be taught by John Bruce at Percy Street Academy in Newcastle, ten miles from his home.

His mother, known as Fanny, had died from tuberculosis and so did his little sister. Because of these sad events in Robert's young life, rather than let him walk ten miles home from Newcastle and worried that he too would catch a cold and die of TB, his father bought him a donkey. Robert became a member of the Newcastle Literary and Philosophical Society. Himself and his father would sit together of a night time and read books on designs and steam engines. They made a sundial together which is still above the door of the old cottage at Long Benton.

After leaving school in 1819 Robert went to work as a mining engineer in Killingworth Colliery. Not being able to purchase a mining compass, he made one, and used it to survey the High Level Bridge in Newcastle. Having not finished his apprenticeship as he showed signs of TB, he was working down West Moor Pit when there was an explosion. Because of this the owner of the pit let Robert go and help his father.

A Scottish engineer had seen potential in Robert and asked his dad if it were ok to send his lad to the University of Cambridge. His dad decided to send him part-time only just for the first year, because he needed his son to help run the business.

Various acts were passed through Parliament and by 1824 Robert Stephenson and Co had been formed to carry out railway surveys and construction and on the 27th September 1825 the Stockton and Darlington railway was opened, transferring coal from Bishop Auckland to Stockton-On-Tees. Robert and his dad were the chief engineers and were responsible for Parliamentary business. Joining the business, also as a chief engineer, was Joseph Locke who had been a major pioneer of railway projects.

In 1829 Robert Stephenson with the help of his dad George and Joseph Locke built Rocket, at the Forth Street Works in Newcastle upon Tyne. It was not the first locomotive to be built, but the locomotive Rocket was a piece of excellence - winning a competition at the Rainhill Trials that had been organised by the Liverpool and Manchester Railway Company.

Rocket had been built specifically to transport not only freight and goods but also passengers. It was classed as 'Rolling Stock' - wheeled vehicles that would travel on rails.

Ascending through hills and dales and over mountains, then down through the vales, Rocket thundered at a speed of thirty six miles per hour, carrying smiling mums, dads and children, all full of gorgeous smiles. Transporting goods, passengers and freight along the double tracks, the most advanced locomotive of its day. Powered by steam, running on two powered driving wheels. A system of classifying where the driving wheels are coupled. Followed by two trailing wheels fast and light cylinders at one time were above the firebox. Locke suggested that the cylinders should be placed below the firebox laying horizontal. The fireman and the driver share a foot plate at the rear.

The sisters of Rocket, all built by the company, Meteor, Comet, Dart, Arrow, North Star, Majestic and the Phoenix all had their cylinders set low.

George died of pleurisy at mid-day on the 12th August 1848. Robert Stephenson died 12th October 1859. Joseph Locke died 18th September 1860. All worked for the benefit of mankind on steam, engines, bridges all great civil engineers of their times.

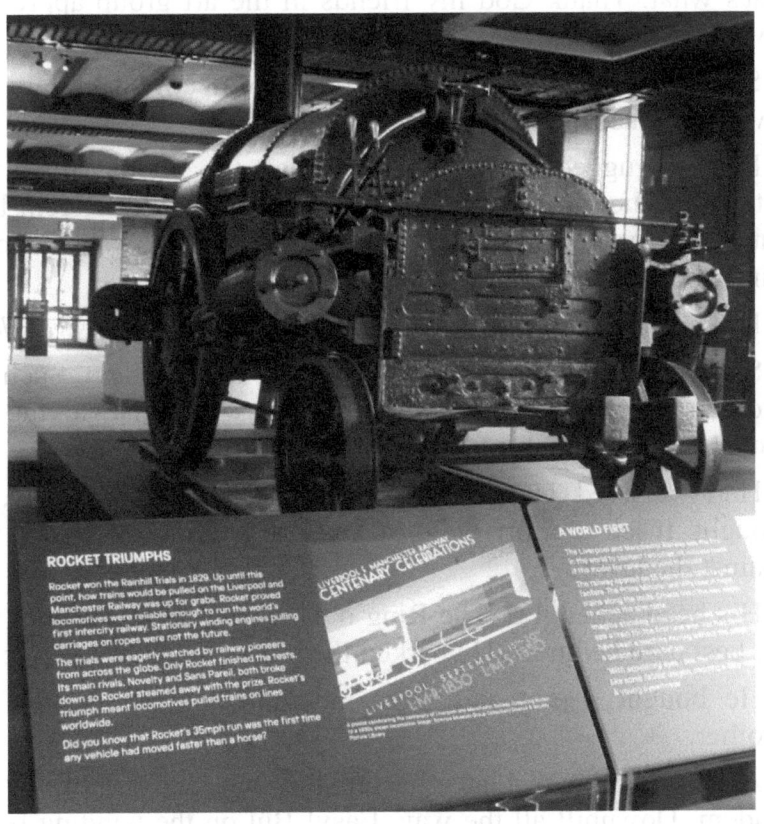

ROCKET TRIUMPHS

Rocket won the Rainhill Trials in 1829. Up until this point, how trains would be pulled on the Liverpool and Manchester Railway was up for grabs. Rocket proved locomotives were reliable enough to run the world's first intercity railway. Stationary winding engines pulling carriages on ropes were not the future.

The trials were eagerly watched by railway pioneers from across the globe. Only Rocket finished the tests. Its main rivals, Novelty and Sans Pareil, both broke down so Rocket steamed away with the prize. Rocket's triumph meant locomotives pulled trains on lines worldwide.

Did you know that Rocket's 35mph run was the first time any vehicle had moved faster than a horse?

A Bicycle Made for Two

ANNE WINNARD

Helen signed her painting with a flourish.

'A masterpiece!' she declared.

Harry seemed unconvinced. 'If you say so.'

'Oh, go to hell Harry. What do you know about art? Nothing, that's what. Thank God my friends in the art group appreciate my work.'

She had recently entered a piece in a competition, certain that it would be accepted.

Harry shrugged his shoulders and left the studio, which was actually a shed in the garden. He dragged the old tandem bike out of the garage and set off towards the village. It was an uphill climb, but in second gear it soon became easier.

He sang an old song, *Daisy, Daisy, give me your answer do.*

So many happy hours they had spent on the tandem. Such joy and fun. Then Helen had found she was an artist, loving the flattery and adulation of her artist friends.

Harry arrived at a fork. Which road? Not that way, he thought. It led to a private estate, and travelling through it was against the law.

His head ached, but The Ring o' Bells lay ahead. Within was the best cure he knew. He parked the tandem outside the pub.

He bought a pint and then one more and another -- and another.

A couple of hours later he left the pub, and set off on the tandem. Downhill all the way. Easy! But on the winding bends of the hill, he lost control. The brakes failed completely and he was hurled head first into a tree.

Later Helen was sitting by his bed. Would he ever waken? Why had she been so nasty to him? She had shown no interest in him at all. Seeing the mangled tandem had brought back memories of all their good times.

Not long after she had sent him out, she had been informed by text that her competition entry had not been accepted - and worse still, funding had been withdrawn for the art class.

She had never felt so lonely. The voice in her head said 'Please come back. There's still so much we can do together.'

Harry's eyelids fluttered. He was waking up. He opened his eyes. My God he had a headache, but was overcome with happiness. He burst into song, singing the last two lines of the old lyric,

But you'll look sweet, upon the seat,

of a bicycle made for two.

Book Heaven

BARRY SEDDON

On a hot summer holiday in Northumberland, my wife and I went looking for a bookshop and found a reader's paradise.

In the enchanting town of Alnwick, where the castle would one day be the setting for Harry Potter's college of magic, a farmer recommended we visit Barter Books. A quarter mile from the cobbled market square, we found a solid Victorian-style building.

It looked like no bookshop we'd ever seen, but in it we found magic of a very different kind to J K Rowling's. Barter Books was a converted railway station. We visited twice more and after that it was always the icing on our holiday cake.

Barter Books is still there, open 10 hours a day, seven days a week, except for Christmas Day. There is also an enchanted and appropriate extra for boys of all ages -- a huge model railway with three tracks weaving under and over each other, all around the largest room.

There are several things to love about Barter Books. Apart from its mountains of books on hundreds of yards of shelves, it has a cosy buffet with a welcoming fire, homely hot food, scones, tea, coffee, occasional cream cakes and comfortable old armchairs where no-one complains if you just sit and read.

The staff play a large part in the success of this unique venture. All are hard-working and loyal. They're mainly temps, as young as 16 and as old as 76, from numerous backgrounds, from teachers to coal miners. You can hear accents from everywhere, the North of England, Ireland, London, Cornwall, even America.

It started in April 1991, when Missouri-born Mary Manley, needing to deal with a rather large overdraft, decided to open a second-hand bookshop, based on the swap system. Her husband Stuart suggested that she use the front room of his small manufacturing plant within the station. And from that seed grew what the *New Statesman* would later call, without exaggeration, "The British Library of second-hand bookshops."

Now Stuart looks after general business and the website, while Mary's province is organisation, marketing and the Barter Books ambience, with the station setting at its root.

The splendid building was designed by William Bell in 1887 and at 32,000 square feet is remarkably large for a small market town. The explanation is that Alnwick is the seat of the Dukes of Northumberland and in the 19th Century a grand station was deemed necessary to impress visiting royalty.

History was not always kind however. Dr Beeching's axe fell in 1968 and the station died. It was 23 years before fortune smiled again, when Mary and Stuart took over. Then one day in 2008 another chapter began. More space was needed and the shop manager discovered a large derelict room, "lost" for 30 years, deep in dust and cobwebs and with an ancient fern clinging to life under a dripping pipe. That room became the station buffet, which is now the cosy hub of Barter Books.

The original station canopy has been restored, all the fireplaces work, children have a space of their own, books on subjects from Renaissance architecture to science fiction are waiting to be bartered, and public life has been restored to a building that was made for it.

Meanwhile, dedicated railway volunteers are restoring two local branch lines. They've called it the Aln Valley Railway. Stuart and Mary's dream is to see an engine steam back in along one of those lines. Then they themselves can relax, sit by one of their fires and read a book. Perhaps.

The Lock-In

BILL CAMERON

In a quiet corner of The House of Hops sat a young couple, Laura and Vince, dawdling over a cup of coffee and a pint of Kentucky Riot craft stout from a local brewery Beatnikz. The tap room might have seemed an odd venue for the lovers on a Saturday night. Early closing, beer and coffee would not generally be an attraction for youngsters like these. More usually they would be part of a noisy company of lager-swilling youths like the dozen or so in the back room, drinking the Münchner Hell German lager before heading off for a night on the town. This, however, was the perfect place to while away a couple of hours before going back early to her parents' couch to spend the rest of the evening in front of the TV with the lights out.

'I like it in here, don't you?' said Vince, smiling, 'My Dad told me about it. It reminds me of the atmosphere of my Grandma's front parlour.'

Not lifting her eyes, which seemed fixated on the latte before her, Laura muttered, 'Suppose it's OK. A bit dead though ain't it? No Karaoke, no TV, no pool table, no fruit machines – just a lot of boozers.'

'Aw, come on love, don't be so miserable. 'What's up with you tonight?'

'Nothing.' A classic answer, saying nothing but declaring a lot more unsaid beneath that single word.

'Look around Laura. What we have here, you won't see in your regular pubs. There's that couple from down your street, playing Scrabble with some friends. Probably enjoying some relief from the kids for an hour or so and not getting home late.'

156

'Looks boring to me.' She wasn't being drawn into a discussion.

'And don't you think there's some characters in those three old blokes in the corner. I saw them sampling the range of craft beers before ordering – you won't get that in the local. Connoisseurs every one of 'em. Not like the lager drinkers we usually hang around. Are you sure nowt's wrong?'

'They're just hardened boozers, laughing at their own stupid jokes. They'll be going home for Match of the Day soon. When does this place close?'

'My Dad comes in regularly through the week with his mate. He says *last orders* is eight o'clock. It's half seven now so we've time for another drink and then we'll go back to yours before your Mam and Dad get back from the Legion.'

'Suppose so.'

They sat in the homely tap room of the beer shop holding hands but not saying much, satisfied to take in the warm ambience and jolly regulars. Vince tried to liven up the conversation, pointing out the quirky characters. People-watching was far better than TV. His girl-friend, however, could not be coaxed into more than a sigh and bland comment.

They finished their drinks as the clock showed half past eight. They were puzzled that there had been no great exodus and the bar was still serving.

'Are you ready to go now? I'll take you home if you don't want my company.' He was trying to rationalise her aloofness tonight. 'Probably a *woman's thing*', he told himself, She'll be OK tomorrow.'

'I thought you said this place closes at eight o'clock. I don't feel like going home. . Is this what they call a lock-in?'

'Looks like it. No escape for us yet. What do you want to drink then?'

She chose from the 4 Sisters Salford distillery gins on offer - a strawberry blend with ice and tonic. Proprietor Scott took Vince through samples of three different craft beers, from which he chose a pint of South Pacific New Zealand Pale Ale provided by the small Blackedge brewery in Horwich. They returned to the round table by the cold bottled and canned drinks cabinet and settled down again.

'Enjoy your gin – cheers!' Vincent saluted, 'Cheer up! It's not the end of the world.'

A tear rolled down the young girl's cheek. 'I'm sorry Vince; I'm just not good company tonight.' She sighed. He knows there is more to follow. His heart stumbled. He'd been dumped before, but this time he wasn't prepared for it nor prepared to give up without a fight. Only as the thought crashed his mind did he realise what she meant to him.

'Vince?'

His grim look found the floor, 'Yeh?'

'Vince, you're a really nice guy but...'

He interrupted, 'Don't drop me Laura We've been going together for nearly a year now. If you want to move on, let's at least keep being friends,' - clutching at the only emotional straw he could reach.

'Vince, I don't want to be a burden on you and it's my fault as much as yours.'

He said he was puzzled and wanted to know what she was getting at.

'Vinnie, I'm pregnant.'

At the whispered admission, his jaw dropped. The realisation hit him like a sledgehammer. A bombshell, but what a wonderful bombshell of opportunity. His first instinct was purely selfish. Now he would have to stick by her and she would be stuck with him, wouldn't she?

But she was talking...

'Vince, I think you should move on. We're only young once and I don't want to tie you down. You're a nice lad and you can enjoy yourself for years without being lumbered with me. I won't blame you if you want to leave me.'

In spite of her caution the news was the catalyst for an action he had contemplated many times recently, but it had never been the 'right moment'. Leaving Laura would, he told himself, open the oyster of the world to adventure. But it could be the greatest regret of his life. He went with his heart.

It's surprising that very often circumstances conspire to introduce a hiatus in the background clamour of people enjoying their leisure. In a quiet corner of a quiet pub on a quiet street a young man dropped to his knees and smiled an irresistible smile, 'That's fantastic news. Marry me Laura.'

'Yes. Oh yes please.' Her face glowed with joyful radiance as the gloom lifted. With encouragement from Claire behind the bar, the room applauded and that same face glowed with embarrassed pink.

They saw out the lock-in with a few more drinks to celebrate their engagement with new-found friends in the tap room. On asking about the lock-in they were told that the eight o'clock curfew was the weekday licence and Saturday *last orders* was extended to nine o'clock. They left the House of Hops when it closed and then called round to the Legion to surprise her parents with the news.

Footnote:

OTHER CRAFT BEERS AND GINS ARE OFFERED AT THE TAP ROOM FROM TIME TO TIME. THIS STORY IS MERELY A REPRESENTATION OF ONE DAY'S FARE.

Alderly Forest

A full moon in a grey and misty sky,
Looking down through the tall willow branches,
A wavy line of shivering shadows moved hand in hand,
Towards the clearing. Eyes glittering by and by.

Darkness as the clouds moved slowly over the smiling moon,
Witches and wizards watched intently, discreetly,
As their little ones, twelve in total, three to the south,
three to the north, three to the west and three the east, soon.

They had a mission, as their ancestors had before,
An acorn and stick in each little hand,
The outer shadow of the north, south, east and west,
Gently placed their baby oak in a hole that had been dug
before,

Pointed end down, then covered it with blessed soil,
Sacred singing voices filled the cold foggy night,
The circle moved to the left, the first child moved to the centre.
Another acorn placed with gentle fingers north, south, east and
west, recoil.

160

The circle moved to the left once again, and four shadowy fingers buried more.

As dawn broke and the crows stretched their wings and flew,

Twelve acorns placed, the circle complete.

200 hundred years have flown by. deep beneath the forest floor.

Thousands of tiny roots have joined hidden fingers and hidden hands,

And above ground stands a mighty oak

Witches and wizards protect the mighty oak of years gone by.

The crows return to roost, laughter of children, mystic voices of distant lands.

LILLIAN HASSALL

161

Two Chimneys, One Cat and Lots of Crows

BARRY SEDDON

Both holidays should have been wonderful. They were – eventually. But the idylls, in Shropshire and on Anglesey, worthy of H.E. Bates at his most bucolic, became settings for dread and fear. That's the way we tell it anyway. Dined out on it a few times I can tell you.

The first longed-for break was in Shropshire, a country mile or so from Whitchurch, down a vertiginous lane seemingly carved from the side of a red sandstone cliff. The children loved it.

I swear our ancient Austin Cambridge gave me a baleful stare when we came to a spring-rocking halt and I strove to bend my white knuckles back to more or less normal. That took an hour, during which I drank three mugs of almost black coffee and Marjorie completely unpacked the boot. Aren't women wonderful?

When I asked why she was so calm Marjorie explained that she had closed her eyes and prayed from the moment we went over the cliff edge. Funny, when we went to inspect it later, the lane seemed not half as terrifying. Just many times steeper than anything you'll find in Salford – including The Brow at Worsley!

After one or two pointed hints (well, probably three or four) I helped with the rest of the unpacking. The cottage had been the roomy home of a small-holder, his wife, a grandmother and a brood of kids. It was a farmhouse from the late 1800s, stone-built to last forever -- and BIG.

162

Which was just as well because Marjorie had brought enough food to feed Napoleon's army, with crockery and cutlery to match and even some furniture. None of it needed of course, because my workmate Jim and his wife, who owned and let the place, had left it fully stocked. There were even push-bikes for Colin and Helen and deck-chairs for us. I gave Marjorie a meaningful look and dodged what could have been a painful kick on the shin.

First day over, however, it turned into a wonderful fortnight. We went to a country market at what seemed like dawn, where 32-piece tea-sets from the Potteries sold for almost nothing; we had picnics in Happy Valley, on our way to the wonderful Hodnet Hall and Gardens; we made friends with the Williams farming family at Wem and brought home a grey kitten; we talked to huntsmen in full red regalia, a dog pack and a horn they let us all try; and we sampled the wonders of a country fair, where Helen walked UNDER a Shire horse and we bought a stool with a seat of woven hemp that is still being used.

So yes...wonderful, except for one day in the middle. It started wet, progressed to worse and got really cold. Colin found a note held down by a stone on the hearth. 'Great!' he shouted. 'It says we can light a fire!'

We did. Quite proud of it we were -- crumpled copies of the Telegraph, sticks from a woodshed at the back, light the white touch-paper and stand clear.

It caught beautifully. We cheered. Then cheers changed to coughs as the room filled with smoke. There must be a blockage in the chimney! With the fire damped down I phoned Jim.

He laughed. 'Don't worry, you're the first guests this year. It's the crows. Every year they build those stupid big nests of criss-crossed sticks on top of the chimney, hatch the chicks, then clear off. The sticks fall down and block the chimney.'

163

'So what do we do?' I asked plaintively (I've often wondered what plaintiff sounded like...). 'Is there a chimney sweep nearby?'

'No. Too expensive – and they don't like the lane. So it's a DIY job. Just stick four or five sheets of the Telegraph up the flue. Then another one that you've lit. That'll shift it. Never fails.'

'Well thanks,' I said. 'I suppose...'

Jim laughed again. 'Just one thing .... don't worry if it roars a bit.'" Click, and he was gone.

The kids jumped up and down with excitement. Marjorie gave me one of those Looks... She knows me well.

What neither of us knew was that the crows had been extra busy that year, building nest after stupid nest, filling the flue to the brim. The twigs and branches, kept tinder dry by the natural up-draft, caught and crackled. So far so good....

Then Jim's 'roaring' started. Soon it was deafening and I dashed upstairs to the bedroom. I touched the chimney breast. It was HOT! It was also vibrating like a hammer action drill and the roaring was getting louder by the second.

Back down! Colin and Helen were tribal dancing outside, pointing at the flaming chimney and Marjorie was briskly walking in from the kitchen with a bucket of water. 'This'll fix it,' she said and poured it onto the burning nest debris and the smouldering remains of our first fire.

Steam billowed up the flue, the fire went out, Helen and Colin were sad and Marjorie gave me that Look. I breathed a sigh of relief and went to make a cuppa. Aren't women wonderful?

---oo---

The following year we rented a cottage on Anglesey. It looked like being a blissful break. Only five days, as we'd both used up our holiday allotments but even so.... Marjorie's Mum was looking after the children so it was just the two of us. Oh yes, and Cindy. Cindy, now a full-grown cat, but just as kittenish, was in her basket on the back seat of the car, parked around the side. She didn't travel well, so we'd given her a sedative.

Just as well, it turned out. When Glenda Jones, the neat little spinster who owned the cottage came to greet us, we were admiring the pale straw-coloured carpet. 'Yes, it's lovely,' she agreed. 'I daren't tell you how much it cost. Let's just say I'm glad I have the no pets rule.' She glanced around. 'You obviously saw it in my letter. Do you have pets at home?'

'Of course,' said Marjorie and my heart sank, 'but Mum takes care of things.'

I breathed out as they went into the garden, chattering of this and that. What the hell should we do?

'Got to let Cindy in for a while,' said Marjorie, 'then she'll have to live in the back garden. Thank goodness the weather's fine and that we're only here for five days. I'll go and get her now.'

She returned, cuddling our sleepy grey-haired pet, who suddenly woke, raring to go, leaped out of her arms and disappeared up the chimney at 60 miles an hour. Then she reappeared, sneezing soot and bounced out to the kitchen.

Marjorie hurtled after her, gave her a full tin of cat food with another sedative pill and we were delicately wafting away the last of 42 black footprints on the gorgeous straw-coloured carpet when the doorbell rang again.

'Yoo-hoo!' said Glenda Jones. 'I've brought some milk in case you had none.' Marjorie, quick-thinking as ever, took it, thanked her and led her back into the garden to talk about geraniums.

We survived the holiday. Enjoyed it too. Especially after the second day. We'd called for some eggs at a local farm. The farmer fully understood Marjorie's winsome tale of Miss Jones's carpet and said he'd take good care of Cindy for the rest of our holiday.

'Oh, would you? Really?' said Marjorie and smiled her Smile, which was just as effective as her Look. 'Yes,' said the blushing farmer. His children had always wanted a pet and Cindy would fill the gap perfectly, ...'like a sort of trial.'

Marjorie left one of her coats as a comfort blanket for Cindy and we picked her up on the way home. As I said earlier: Aren't women wonderful?

A Lonely Tree

My trunk is gnarled now, it wasn't always so;
my leaves are my dress so to speak
and very 'Vivienne Westwood' don't you think?
There is so much space around me,
I wish it were not so, I long for company.
He didn't think about that when he planted me all those years
ago.
How could he know how lonely I would be?
I eavesdrop on all the conversations of the people who sit
beneath my branches.
Lovers, who shouldn't be.
Would-be mothers who couldn't be.
Sad people, glad people.
Bad and mad people.
Venting their self-centred chatter, but I listen and wait, as my
friendless future stretches endlessly before me.
Who cares? Nobody. I am only a tree.
AUDREY EDWARDS

167

The Rose

It seems so long ago when you put me
In the ground; when we were young,
With time enough to grow.

You fed and watered me, protected me,
From the harsh frost, helped me to be
Healthy and strong like you.

168

I loved when you gently felt my petals
As soft as velvet to your touch,
As if we were in love.

I loved the long, hot summers without rain,
When you quenched my thirst with water
To show how much you cared.

I loved it when you leaned, breathed in deeply,
Smelled the perfume that I gave you,
Smiled to show your pleasure

I loved it when you watched me gaily dance
To the haunting music of the wind,
And sometimes, you joined in.

I loved it too, when your red silk dress,
Brushed against my rich, ruby hues,
To blend ourselves as one.

We've survived the changes of the seasons,
Comforted each other through times
When dark clouds have threatened.

SWit'CH

This summer I have watched you growing frail,
Feared that you would soon have to go,
And leave me weak and empty.

You have not smelled my perfume for a while,
Nor felt my petals tenderly,
Nor beamed your gentle smile.

Now you are not here and I am thirsty,
Without rain, without you. I know,
I will see you no more.

I sense that you are going far away,
A place where I can never go,
That you are almost there.

I feel it: float my petals to the ground,
From whence I came, where, together,
We both die and wither

SYLVIA EDWARDS

170

Under the Bush

BARRY SEDDON

I was only 16 and a bit of a nerd when a very interesting event under a rhododendron bush left me feeling a fair bit older and a lot less innocent. For such an important occasion, it started quite prosaically with a visit to a garden centre, to choose a present for Mum and Dad. It ended with a vivid lesson scrawled across the blank slate of my life, leaving little room for computer games.

It was almost closing time. The crowds were drifting to the check-outs when I met my *teacher*, a young assistant in the flowering shrubs area. She was about 20, with hair like a drifting red aurora and a figure that gave me flutters in regions where blushes are born. I began to feel that I'd happily die for her as long as that body was pressed close to mine.

Before buying, I wanted to know why some of our back-garden bushes were dying, particularly the rhododendron. Melissa, for that was her lovely name, asked where the plant was and when I said 'in a sheltered corner,' she laughed. 'That's why!' she said. 'Come on, I'll show you' and led me, crouching, between the tangled stems of an ancient rhododendron.

It was almost dark. I stumbled over a root and she grabbed my arm and steadied me. Somehow, we drifted closer and she began to tell me all about the mating habits of certain garden pests. Her breath was delightfully warm on my cheek. 'They get everywhere with their feelers before laying their eggs,' she said.

'How do you mean?' I asked, beginning to tremble.

So she showed me.

171

Trees

BARRY SEDDON

Trees are time's children, living in an ever-changing bubble, blown for them to live in: exulting in summer sunshine; drooping in failing autumn light, shedding strips of silver bark and crisping leaves; sleeping under warm white winter blankets until time turns the earth, springing them awake to days of running sap and climbing boys.

Oak, beech, chestnut, sycamore and lime, cousins, sisters, brothers, talking to each other when their questing rootlets touch, living in their baubles of joy that hold a mirror to the world. Time is full of gifts for her children: plumped-up cloud blankets under which to snuggle, sunshine in which to bask and grow; rain to cleanse them, frost to pin them with silver party favours. She is their comfort-friend.

FINALIST 2018 NAWG COMP: – MONOLOGUE

Door

SYLVIA EDWARDS

I touch your smooth hardness again. Run my fingers down your erect spine. Pull. But still you fail to move. Then I try once more... hesitate... just for a second... imploring you... to respond... and open up to me. At last - you do, reluctantly. I sigh, but still hold on to your safety. The solid, reassuring permanence of your shape. Thank you. Thank you, for being simply - there! I know that you hear me.

I peep beyond the confines of your refuge, not yet able to let go of your strength: my shield. Now, the street assaults my ears like an orchestra tuning. Do you hear it: this distorted barrage of life - that was once sweet music to my ears. Boots tap! A dog barks! Car doors bang like bombs. Children shriek! A motorbike roars. People jostle this way and that. I know you hear it too. Only you can feel me tremble - then freeze. I feel your tentacles reaching out - to pull me back to safety. Thank you. Thank you, door. As you close silently - all is quiet once again. We breathe deeply, you and I. But now I wonder; are you my jailer in disguise? Or my means of escape? Or, are we now so bonded that I will never know? Perhaps I can never leave you. Are you my silent partner - for life?

But, door, did you also feel it - out there? Did you also brace yourself against the wind? Hear the shouts? And smell the fumes? Did you also see the strangers? So many strangers. Watching both of us. Waiting to pounce. You understand, don't you? You know I am not as mad as I sound. Only you know that life on the other side of you is, to me, as distant as a journey to the moon. And only you know why. Because you... only you... have seen the real me.

See how my tears now gush like a waterfall down a rocky mountainside. See how I weep uncontrollably, uncaring what you think. Do you feel the wetness of my fingers, as they meander down your smooth, varnished surface, until I humbly kneel before you - as if before a sacred altar? But prayers will not work for me.

Look at you! I know you better than any human. I see you daily - study you as you watch me, stroke your rectangular, symmetrical contours. Sometimes you are warmed by the radiator that is your constant companion. At others, you are cold, through the darkness of the night, in the depth of winter, when the heating is off - and the world is stark and white.

Only your mouth speaks. The silent messenger. Each morning I wait to see your brass lips open, then swiftly close, spewing out the messages that still lie, unopened beside you on the hall table - gathering the dust of time. Do you know what is in them? Are you happy in your role, standing guard? Controlling contact with that other world where people watch and wait - to separate us? To hurt me? But you are strong and sturdy. I trust you as I trust no other. I know that you will protect me from what is out there - and from myself!

It's Monday. But you know that. You watched me mark this new day off my calendar this morning, after having waited all yesterday for a new day to come. You watched me and wondered if this day would be different than the rest. Tomorrow, you will let Elsie in. Only Elsie. You know that it's okay. You will let her in, and wait, while she drops the shopping down on the porch floor, asks how I am, then leaves - as she has always done. Then you will close... to lock me inside my cell once more. My jailer! Are you not ashamed to have that role?

How long has it been? Days? Weeks? Months? No, years. Thousands of painful days when I have spent my time staring at you. Now I'm sick of seeing you standing there in the same place - blocking my way to freedom. But you know, don't you. Because you're as sick of me as I am of you!

I can't bear to touch you anymore. So I stand and move away... force myself to meet my eyes in the hall mirror, though I see that you watch me still. The face that gazes back at me is not yet mine. It is a stranger's face, although I have tried to accept it. My new face - glued on like a mask of papier-mâché - rough and hard to my touch. It is a face the outside world has yet to see - and I am afraid. But you know that, don't you? Every day - as I beg you to let me out. You, only you, have yet glimpsed the new me.

You alone know that photo haunts me still? We see it every day. The shimmering whiteness of my veil and bridal gown taunts us both. I long to hit you with it. Shall I? Shall I throw it at you? Watch me! There! I have done it! Do you hear the glass shatter against the surface of your hard heart? Just like my own heart that now lies in a million pieces! Do you?

Enough! I know you can hear me, breathing deeply as I try again, as I have, to open you. Do you not feel my fingers gripping hard? Pleading with you? But still you will not move. You win! Watch me, as I unwind my scarf... take off my hat. Lastly, the dark glasses. You stand brighter now - sunlight strengthens you. I stand before you, stripped of my disguise, strangely vulnerable. What are you thinking as you watch me run shaking fingers through these wispy remnants of what was once hair - before the acid attack? Do you feel anything?

Our daily battle is over now ... and you have won. A truce!

But tomorrow is another day!

Seasons

Through frigid winter air,
Silent and without pause they fall.
Catch them if you can,
You'll always fail
To seize the snowflakes whitening your walls

Comes the green life springing,
Pushing through the slowly-warming earth.
While deep within the
Snow drop stems,
Tight-folded flowers wait upon their birth

Now come the lemming crowds,
Racing through the heat to summer sea,
While grassy tides roll
Gently in, through
Drowsing fields of butterfly and bee

Cooling trees slow down their sap
And autumn wind spills leaves upon the ground
The days grow short
And darkness falls,
To shade the earth till spring should come around

BARRY SEDDON

Decline and Fall

ALAN RICK

From office cleaner to starry-eyed exotic dancer – this was a spectacular leap to be sure. Her first job on leaving school was in a factory making tooth brushes. Her relentless daily task was to bore a hole in each toothbrush as it passed before her on a moving belt. She declared it to her parents as exciting work and proudly announced at the end of her first week that she had bored 3708 holes that week.

Her parents were underwhelmed by this news but declared that 'the lass has to start somewhere.' From this lowly occupation she passed to a succession of less lowly jobs until she arrived via a course in dancing at a local performing arts school. She then decided that the role of exotic dancer was the future she was destined for and assumed the exotic name of Natasha Swaroski who sounded like a dancer from the Bolshoi in Moscow. Well it was much more exotic than her real name which was Jane. Ultimately she opened her own dancing school The Bolshoi Belles.

It was not in an actual studio but in her mum's sitting room - as her parents had said the lass had to start somewhere. At last she received the news that she was to give a dance demonstration in The Leeds Gallery as part of an open competition of local dancing. A prize and contract would be awarded to the winner.

Jane surveyed herself in the mirror. She had to make sure that everything was in order for the dancing demonstration she had to give in the Leeds Gallery that afternoon. Her newly formed dance academy – Proprietor Natasha Swaroski – all types of dancing taught – would receive a tremendous boost if she could dazzle the invited audience with a virtuoso display. All was right – hair expensively permed to keep it in place while performing, court shoes polished to see your face in, and a stratospherically priced dress that would have given her bank manager heart failure if only she had told him about it. But what was expense when the future of the academy was at stake?

Arriving at the gallery – chosen as the venue because of its highly polished floor – Jane took a look at the serried ranks of the audience seated on both sides of the floor. Here were weighty denizens of the world of dancing – a solid block of potentially fierce critics who would give no quarter if the demonstration was not up to standard.

To a soft ripple of encouraging applause Jane slunk into an arabesque – a suitable dance to begin with, being slow and sensual. Looking round at the faces, Jane sensed admiration all around her. Oohs and Aahs floated on the air like soap bubbles – then melted away. Time to push the boat out and thrill them with something frenzied and vigorous and, to their amazement she suddenly flung herself into the wild abandon of the Hungarian czardas. Startled cries rent the air – frantic scribbles in notebooks accompanied the looks of wonder on the faces on all sides.

"It's a triumph," glowed Jane to herself, as she took in the surroundings, "This is going to put the academy on the map without a doubt"

Intoxicated by the heady wine of fame that surely beckoned now, she twisted, pirouetted and lunged like a manic doll just released from all restraint. "No more foxtrots and sedate waltzes for me." She purred as the unbridled power of success took over her mind. Both she and the music drove on to a wild climax until, quite suddenly, she found herself not on the map, but on the floor – a tangled mass of legs, skirt and lost dignity.

The silence was not golden – her moment not limelit – the air not frenzied - but dull and flat. Dare she look now? At last she did and found herself staring at row after row of empty seats.

How transient are drunken thoughts of fame – one moment kindled into a furnace – the next doused with a hose.

A Load of Bull

ROSEMARY SWIFT

Maisie's first dinner party had gone well. As a newlywed in her pristine home on a desirable housing estate she had been eager to host it for her husband's sake. From monies given to her by an indulgent Aunt as a wedding gift, her husband had recently bought into the Law Firm where he had been a Solicitor for the past ten years and now as a junior partner it was an unspoken requisite to host such a gathering.

The other three partners and their wives were not to know that her Mum had slaved for her in the kitchen and now, the meal over, they were sitting around the table playing a parlour game; the one where a name or phrase was placed on your forehead and you had to guess what it was. Maisie had chosen to go first to get it over with, as although she was anxious to please she had never played it before. She knew that it was customary to suggest what it could be from general clues provided but those present seemed to want to play by their own rules.

"Oh, do you remember, darling when we were last in Spain" said one of the wives "and that matador was eyeing me up; you were jealous so I didn't dare buy a souvenir of his prey."

Everybody burst out laughing as Maisie just looked blankly about. Her husband cast a frown and drank deeply from his glass of red wine, the latest of many he had already imbibed which she had put down to nerves.

"Well, dear, you could have had it for your birthday, I suppose," a senior partner guffawed, "After all it would have been apt for your birthday sign in late May."

Everybody laughed merrily; again Maisie did not twig, and again her husband drank deeply.

"I can remember my dear old Northern Grandfather telling me of how when they drove the cattle down the road from the railway sidings to the abattoir he once saw a cow make a run for it into the open door of a public house – I wonder if it was called the Black ......erm" said the office joker (promoted out of turn before her husband because as her husband would darkly say he kept them all amused.)

Everybody roared with laughter but again she did not catch on and by now her husband was looking quite apoplectic.

A very serious lady known for her intellectual leanings, looked at her kindly:

"Prior to the Papal Brief which came into use as a less formal means of communication in 14th century there used to be a Papal erm."

This time everybody looked blank apart from the learned lady's husband, the most senior of the partners, who smiled benignly.

The office joker so as to lighten the mood butted in again and said about how the same old Northern Grandfather had told him about going in the Black *you-know-what* and playing darts on a Manchester Board which was much smaller in diameter than the London Board now more commonly used, so it was much harder to hit the outer never mind the inner *you-know-what* of the Board.

Everybody laughed hilariously and as Maisie looked across at her husband with pleading eyes, she saw he was puce in colour as he jumped up suddenly, bringing with him the red-coloured damask tablecloth containing the whisky, port and sherry decanters (old-fashioned of course but, as they had been a wedding gift from the Law Firm, had been put to use).

The office joker grabbed the cloth and pranced around the room enacting the gestures of a matador but this time nobody laughed along with him.

"Oh, darling" said Maisie to her husband "be careful – you are like a bull in a china shop."

"No, you stupid cow - that is what you are... a Bull, a bloody Bull."

He snatched the sticky label from her brow and thrust it at her to read. Just four short letters B U L L – her very brand-new surname.

Silence descended, and after an uncomfortable moment or so, one or two mooted that it was time to go - and off they all went saying see you next time at wherever it would happen to be. But Maisie knew and her husband knew that an invitation for them would not be forthcoming.

One More Day

Just another day to get through - it's not easy, my dear heart.

God knows how hard it's been for me, since the day we had to part.

I hate each day without you.

Nothing can me please, it's just another day I wish would quickly cease.

Another day to get through: try, try, try.

Fill my time with endless chores to make the hours go by.

Morning comes too soon for me. I have to wake alas and spend my time, another day, with fake smiles and morass.

The candles on my birthday cake - put out every one. For now one year has slowly passed since last time they were blown.

One full year my darling, I haven't seen your face or touched your hair or held your hand or felt your warm embrace.

Nothing makes sense any more - why would it without you?

Just another day to fill and hope I will get through.

Just another day.

AUDREY EDWARDS

Wallflower

BILL CAMERON

"So why aren't you dancing?"

The confrontational tone of this challenge tore Lucy out of her reverie. As usual, she found herself seated alone nursing a bottle of Coke listening to the music and tapping along to the rock 'n' roll rhythm. Her friends were all paired off jiving wildly under the mirror ball.

"Well," she thought, "At least he's speaking directly to me, not over my head to a *does-she-take-sugar?* surrogate."

Lucy took her time composing an answer less sarcastic than she felt the question deserved. "I can't. My legs don't work like yours." She ran the coke bottle along the spokes of her chair wheel for emphasis.

He gave her an exaggerated hang-dog sorrowful look and replied with condescending sarcasm, "Aw, you poor miserable darling – and no friends to talk to either. Life is so cruel when you're wheel-chair bound."

You could cut the tension with a knife. He was now getting under her skin. "I'm not miserable – you don't have to dance to enjoy rock 'n' roll. And my friends will be back after this number. In fact we have a great time here every Friday. And you are very, very rude."

"Feisty reaction – that's good." He thought and continued, "You've still not said why you won't dance. How can you just sit there with this music energising your every bone and sinew? My name's Tommy by the way. What's yours?"

The brusque question had her off guard. Lucy gave him her name. He was, she justified, not bad looking and comforting warmth seemed to pour from within through his twinkling blue eyes. A trace of lopsided smile creased the corner of his mouth.

"Well," she thought, "A few minutes conversation could prove interesting - and he isn't patronising."

She said, "Why do you keep banging on about me dancing? Are you trying to get me on the dance floor to be swung round by a whirling dervish? You're not using me for some macho show for your mates."

More remorseful than she had expected, he apologised, "Oh God no! That's not what I was thinking of at all. I was at a gig once and was really impressed by someone in a wheel chair jiving. You know, I bet we could work out a few moves together so you could dance. And I don't mean I'll be throwing you and your chair around all over the place."

She was more than intrigued. "Go on then. Tell me more."

"Well," he said, "In the jive, the girl moves in response to slight touches from her partner. It might look like she's being chucked across the floor, but she's really moving according to signals she's given."

He took her hand. "For example, we hold with finger tips hooked together like this – nothing works if the hold is tighter. If I move my hand so that our palms are touching, it means I'm about to push away, so you will then spin on the spot. So long as you have the music in your head, heart and soul it works a treat. Can you manoeuvre your chair to turn on the spot?"

Lucy answered enthusiastically, "Yes. I've plenty of practice turning in my chair. I played for a wheelchair netball team since I was ten and even won a trophy with a mixed ability team last year. I'll make this machine dance alright!"

"So shall we go outside onto the veranda and practice a few moves. It'll save crashing into everyone on the floor until we get it right." He said as he stood up. "Shall I shove, or are you an independent feminist?"

"No. Please push, that would be nice," she said, happier with his company now.

The music followed them through the French doors onto the dimly lit veranda. Tommy took his new friend through the basic moves, showing with the slightest touch when she ought to turn or move away or close in. With the push handles down now, he could send other messages by a gentle pull or push on her shoulders. They both enjoyed the dance together - with that special thrill that comes with the intimacy of touch. After only a few numbers, they had refined an intuition so that each knew where the partner would be – they invented a few turns that exploited the unique abilities and shapes created by the chair.

"You're better than I could have hoped," said Tommy, "That netball you play has made you a natural."

"Maybe netball partly, but mostly it's having an understanding teacher with a passion for the subject," Lucy answered. Then, "We'd better get back. We've been so intent I forgot my friends.. They'll be wondering where I am."

In the shadows, she could not see the disappointment on his face, nor the almost imperceptible droop of his broad shoulders. His plans had not included an early return to the ballroom. He took her back to her friends where he was introduced and invited to join their party.

"Sorry, I'd love to but have to be somewhere else." he said.

He leaned down to peck Lucy softly on the cheek to the accompaniment of oohs and aahs from her gang.

The disc jockey cut in on the mike with the announcement, "And now boys and girls – the band you've been waiting for.

It's Tommy Gunn and the Bullets, who'll kick off with their interpretation of the Elvis number *Such a Night.*"

"What a night," echoed Lucy when she recognised the lead singer. She sat back enthralled throughout his set. No desire to be dancing now, other than a dream of dancing with him as he sang to her. "At least," she told herself, "he is singing to me."

After seven or eight songs, Tommy took the mike and introduced, "My good friend, Bobby the bass, is a Buddy Holly fan so will give you *True Love Ways* while I get my breath back."

Bobby led off with "Just you know why ..."

Lucy looked up to see Tommy walking towards her.

"So, why aren't you dancing?" he asked as his strong arms lifted her out of the chair. He carried her onto the dancefloor and gently held her close. In the darkened ballroom, under the glittering mirror ball, they waltzed cheek to cheek like millions of lovers have before and will always.

Lucy was no more the wallflower.

187

Career Choices

BILL CAMERON

CHARACTERS
JIM: RETIRED WAKEFIELD COALMINER
CLARE: 15-YEAR-OLD GRANDDAUGHTER
MAVIS: HIS DAUGHTER, CLARE'S MOTHER

JIM SITS IN HIS CAR WAITING OUTSIDE THE HOUSE. MAVIS STANDS AT THE FRONT DOOR OF THE FAMILY HOME.

MAVIS   Come on Clare, your Granddad's waiting for you. Turn your mobile off for just one minute... Have you got your CV? Have you got your school Record of Achievement? I hope you're not going out in those torn jeans again.

(TO JIM)   She'll be along soon. It's just the way kids are nowadays. Can't do anything without twintering all her mates what she's up to. Never a minute away from her sociable mediums. Thanks, by the way, for taking her to the careers exhibition for us. Andy couldn't get the time off to take her himself. Let's hope it brings Clare down to earth and she thinks about the future seriously.

CLARE, TAPPING INTO MOBILE PHONE, WALKS PAST HER MOTHER WITHOUT AN ACKNOWLEDGEMENT, LEAVES THE HOUSE AND GETS IN THE CAR.

188

MAVIS: Good luck sweetheart.

CLARE: Hiya, Granddad – y'all right?

JIM: Yeah. Fine what about you? Fasten your seatbelt
           and we'll get going. Are you looking forward to
           leaving school in summer and leaving all your
           friends behind?

CLARE: Yeah. No. I'm good.

JIM: So, Clare, before we get to this jobs market, do you
           have any ideas about what you'll be doing when you
           leave school in the summer?

CLARE: I've got lots of ideas, Granddad. I'm only comin'
           with you today 'cause my Mam wanted it. Anyway,
           it's better for you to take me than my Dad – he'd
           just keep bangin' on about me not taking school
           serious. I'd be OK on my own. I'm not a baby now
           – I can make my own mind up…

           PAUSES TO SEND ANOTHER TEXT MESSAGE

JIM: Can't you leave your phone alone?

CLARE: I'm not like some of my mates whose parents have
           decided that they will go to Sixth Form College and
           then uni. Penny Schular's dad is payin' for extra
           tutorin' so she can go to college. It's a waste of
           money; she'll never be clever enough for owt harder
           than media studies at uni. But she won't need to
           worry about earnin' a livin' with the money her
           Dad's got. I might carry on at college, depends on
           what my mates are doin'. I wish it was the olden
           days when I could've been a call girl.

JIM: Well you know it'll mean a lot of hard work if you're going to get the best from college. And you've not exactly been burning the midnight oil at school have you?

CLARE: I've done OK --- and I wasn't skivin' off all the time like our Denis did when...

JIM (INTERRUPTS) Yes, but look where it got him. He ended up doing odd jobs where he can and selling dodgy DVDs round the pubs. He didn't even have the option to go down t'pit like me and your dad before – you've got to be looking for something better than working yourself to death for the benefit of capitalist bosses.

CLARE: He gets pretty well paid doesn't he? even without a so-called education. But I suppose you all had it bad – fightin' Thatcher and the police an' all that. Do you know, Granddad, my mates think you're a hero cos I told 'em you stood in line at Orgreave?

JIM: At least it's good to see that you've got some political awareness, Clare. But it's not all about money. I'm pleased to see you have some understanding of how things were in the eighties, but it wasn't very heroic. When you get to work you'll see that conflicts are not all black and white. Just make sure you don't end up in a dead-end job like your brother – if you get better grades, you'll have more choices.

CLARE: You're getting' to sound like my Dad now. Anyway, me and Tina have a plan to get together and rent a chair at the hairdresser's and do nails. She's really artistic you know, and everyone has acrylics and diamantes these days so we can make a good livin'. I could have been a call girl in the eighties.

JIM :   Aye, and I bet there's plenty of 15 year old girls planning to get into nail decorating. I can't see the fashion carrying on much longer and then where will you be?

CLARE: We've got an ace back-up plan – we can do tattoos as well. One table would be enough for us both to work on at the same time, so we'd be able to do the job twice as quick as anyone else. And Kevin McCall said the felt tip drawing I did on his calf in the craft lesson was a good as any tattoo.

PAUSES TO CHANGE CD

I suppose the equality opportunities laws would have been needed for me to be a call girl in those days. Women couldn't just do any of a man's work round here.

JIM: I think you ought to be a bit more realistic, there's got to be training and health and safety issues if you're injecting ink under someone's skin. It's not like the pit used to be in Maggie's day when anyone raising a safety issue was branded a left-wing activist. But we don't know what we'll find at this jobs show, do we?

CLARE: I suppose an office job with computers would be OK. I'm good on the laptops in school and my i-pod – do you know I got the second highest Candy Crush score in the whole school last year? Yeh, computers are an option and some people make millions with them don't they? (PAUSE)

CLARE: If I'd been a call girl, would I be very rich? Didn't Grandma fancy doing it?

JIM: Office work and IT ain't the same as playing games or texting on social media. I don't think you will meet any upcoming Mark Zuckerberg, Steve Jobs or Bill Gates at the show today. And it can be very traumatic when you get deep into the rat race. If you want to see how ambition takes souls you should watch the Alan Sugar self-promotion show?

CLARE: You mean th'apprentice? It's rubbish. All them posh southern kids. I couldn't be so bitchy to people. I might fancy working with animals. Animals are OK.

JIM: Your Dad can't take you today because he can't take any time off – so you'll need to be careful what you get into else you'll get exploited like him. It's not just refugees who get drawn into what they call modern slavery you know. You don't want that do you?

CLARE: I know, granddad. I watch more of the news than my mates. They only see the outside world through Instagram and Twitter and social media. I know what's going on.

STOPS TO READ INCOMING MESSAGE ON I-PHONE

Hey, granddad, look at this. Tina's at the careers show and already talking about a job. Said she's getting a coffee with some guy from Plusnet. Sounds like she's thinking of being a call girl, but indoors in a call centre. So, maybe I could still be a call girl even if it is a bit physical and dirty. There must be a chance somewhere. Do you think they have 'em in Leeds.

JIM: No way! I've been trying to tell you about exploitation and modern slavery. You've not been brought up that way. No granddaughter of mine is going into that game. Do you even know what a call girl has to do? And what's that got to do with animals?

CLARE: Of course I know. She's the one who leads th'horse as pulls the call cart around t'streets and then tips t'sack of call down the call 'all. I'd need to build up my muscles a bit but that's OK isn't it? I'd go to the gym a couple of times a week and have a purple spandex leotard and yellow head band and the lot and listen to my i-tunes while I'm pumping iron.

JIM: And the first thing we need to do at this exhibition is find a language school with elocution lessons to get your northern vowels tweaked.

Leaving Ordsall

ROSEMARY SWIFT

CAST:
EDIE SMYTH, MIDDLE-AGED WIDOW IN
WRAP-AROUND PAISLEY PATTERN
PINAFORE AND TURBAN
JACK JONES, HER ELDERLY WIDOWED DAD
- COLLARLESS SHIRT & WAISTCOAT
FRED MIDDLE-AGED FAMILY FRIEND FLAT
CAP, MUFFLER AND OUTDOOR JACKET
VIOLET, MIDDLE-AGED BEST FRIEND OF
EDIE HEADSCARF AND OUTDOOR COAT

SCENE 1 FRONT LIVING ROOM
CURTAINED WINDOW; SMALL 3-PIECE
SUITE; SMALL SIDEBOARD; LIT FIRE IN
FIREPLACE; LOTS OF TEA CHESTS AND
CARDBOARD BOXES FOR THE REMOVAL
VAN; FRONT DOOR WITH DOORMAT IS
OPEN SHOWING DOORSTEP, BUCKET,
SCRUBBING BRUSH, CLOTH AND
STEPLADDERS.
EDIE IS SCRUBBINGS THE FRONT DOOR
STEP.

Female voice (OFFSTAGE) Why are you bothering to donkey-stone the step, Edie?

EDIE: Always clean on a Thursday, shop on a Friday, bake on a Saturday.

Female voice: Well, you won't be shopping tomorrer – doesn't your removal van come at one o'clock to take you to Irlam?"

EDIE: Yes, fish from the Chippy tomorrer – hope we find a good 'un."

EDIE SQUEEZES OUT HER CLOTH AND WIPES DOWN THE BACK OF THE DOOR AND SKIRTING BOARDS.

SCENE 2: KITCHEN

HOOKS ON DOOR HOLDING OUT-OF-DOOR COATS FOR A MAN & WOMAN AND A CANVAS SHOPPING BAG; SMALL SQUARE TABLE WITH A TIN BOX WITH TWO SPINDLY CHAIRS; LIT GRATE WITH WOOD AND COAL IN A SCUTTLE ON THE HEARTH; SMALL DRESSER WITH SMALL BOWL WITH WHITE CLOTH, TEAPOT, PLATES, MUGS, MILK JUG AND SUGAR BOWL. JACK IS SITTING AT THE TABLE TAKING BITS FROM THE TIN. EVERY NOW AND THEN HE RUBS HIS CHEST.
BACK DOOR LATCH LIFTS AND FRED WALKS IN.

FRED: Hi, Jack – I bet you can't believe you're leaving here after so long but these houses will be flattened next week or so. Saying that, the bulldozers have been clearing streets in Ordsall for a number of years now and at least we've been let off the rent for the last fortnight."

JACK PICKS UP AND WAVES RENT BOOKS

JACK: I should think so, Fred – the money the landlord has had from us all these years! These rent books start in 1903 from Joseph Jones to Albert Jones, to me John Jones and now it's the back-end of 1973 and rent always paid as far as I know on the dot.

FRED: Giving your Sunday name there, Jack. I can remember mi Mam getting us kids to keep quiet when the Rent Man come because mi Dad had boozed the money away. Keep them books, you never know.

JACK: Aye, lad but don't suppose I'll need them as we'll now be renting from Salford Council.

FRED: Anyway, do you want to place a bet on the dogs? I'm going to White City tonight. I've had a flutter on the gee-gees and won two shilling & sixpence so the missus can't complain about me going out again.

JACK: Why not, Fred. Put it on no. 4 in sixth race. Here's a shilling for the Tote.

JACK RUMMAGES FOR CASH IN HIS TROUSER POCKET AND HANDS SHILLING COIN TO FRED

FRED: I get you, Jack – 46 being this house number. Well, good luck all round, mate, with your new house and everything. I'll see you before you go. Try not to worry – you're looking peaky.

FRED EXITS AND EDIE ENTERS FROM THE FRONT ROOM.

EDIE: Was that Fred just going?

JACK: Aye, Edie - he's putting a bet on for me tonight – last one I'll be doing for a while, 'til I get to know the ropes in Irlam.

EDIE: You never know, Dad – the Pub's called the Nag's Head – maybe there's a bookie's next door!

PATS HER DAD ON THE HEAD – HE GRABS HER HAND

JACK: You've been a good daughter to me, our Edith, since your Mam died – I still miss her."

EDIE: It's a good job she's gone, Dad... moving from here would've broken her heart.

JACK: Well, it's where we had all you kids and my folk were here before that, going way back – I don't know how they fitted their large broods in here!

EDIE: What have you got in your box of tricks? I thought you were going to have a good old clear out?

JACK: Well, I keep trying; I've just thrown away an HP Agreement for our first telly from Lomax's on Eccles New Road back in 1960 but look at this, the Bible your brother Ronnie carried throughout Burma – he didn't come home but that did. And it's here with one your Mam's brother Alf did bring back from the trenches. They've both been in your Mam's bedside cupboard covered with her hankie. He was a right clever clog, your Uncle Alf – there's a book here with foreign phrases that he took with him to pick up the lingo.

EDIE: Well, he wasn't that clever to escape catching the Spanish Flu in 1919 - was he, Dad?

JACK: No, poor sod. To get over trench feet and then mustard-gassed only to cop it anyway. Do you know

197

that flu carried off more people than World War One did? (SIGHS).

EDIE: Anyway, I've done you some cheese and onion in milk in the oven – it should have a nice skin on it by now. I'll give the stove a wipe down before it's disconnected and that should do.

REACHES FOR A TEA TOWEL AND OPENS THE OVEN DOOR
I'm going to UCP shop for our tea – some tripe for you and cow heel for me, yummy, yummy. (PAUSE) I must admit I'll miss the shops on Regent Road when we move.

TAKES A BOWL FROM THE OVEN. PLACES IT, SPOON AND FORK ON THE TABLE IN FRONT OF JACK. POURS A MUG OF TEA ADDS MILK FROM BOTTLE OF STERILISED

JACK: Ta, lass. This always tasted lovely when we had the open fire and the oven door on the side. If we leave the porridge soaking overnight that will be the last meal ever here. I should think that was the <u>only</u> meal our folks had in the past when times were bad.

EDIE: I might as well go and put some more coal on the front room fire, Dad – if we've got any left tomorrer, next door can have it – anyway, back to mi cleaning and leave you to have your nap after you've ate.

EDIE GOES IN TO THE FROM ROOM

SCENE 3: FRONT LIVING ROOM
EDIE TENDS TO THE FIRE THEN CLIMBS ON A CHAIR AND STARTS TAKING DOWN CURTAINS AND NETS.
JACK NODS OFF IN THE NEXT ROOM

FRONT DOOR OPENS

Violet (OFFSTAGE): Coo, ee – anybody there?

VIOLET ENTERS WEARING HEADSCARF, OUTSIDE COAT, CARRYING A BULGING WHITE PAPER BAG.

EDIE: Come in Violet, I'm going to take these curtains after all. I want new ones where we're going but this material might come in for something."

VIOLET: Well, I thought you were daft in first place leaving them. They would have been fluttering amongst the rubble in a week or so! And what the 'eck are you cleaning the winder for?

EDIE: Just giving a rub with brown paper and vinegar to keep the glass looking shiny for a short while longer. Do you think I should put newspaper up to the winder? I don't want some folk thinking the house is empty.

VIOLET: Well, you are amongst the first to go, Edie from Tyler Street – we don't get the keys for our new place in Little Hulton for another week yet.

EDIE: I wish you'd chosen the Irlam overspill like us, Vi. It's better for us, it being on a direct bus route from family – although I must admit everyone says the new Council Estate in Little Hulton is better laid out. I'll miss you – going through school and working in the mill and being together ever since.

VIOLET: Well, with Harry still at Agecroft it makes sense – he can get the bus better to work. In fact, it should be better getting there than from here. He wasn't happy about us living down in Ordsall when we wed, him being a Swinton lad, but I couldn't leave mi Mam.

EDIE: Well, I'm glad you did stay here. My Frank and your Harry were good pals until my Frank was took from me.

VIOLET: Harry misses being with Frank when he walks over Trafford Bridge on a Saturday to watch United.

EDIE: He'll have to start watching Bolton Wanderers!

VIOLET: That would be all...! I hear there's a good Social Club on Armitage Lane – they have live Acts on a Saturday. Remember the times we treated ourselves to Salford Hippodrome and then on to the Salisbury on Trafford Road, that bit posher and a nice change from being in the snug at The Amalgamated.

EDIE: I'll miss our sing-songs, especially when you used to sing 'Rose of England' – you were better than Vera Lynn, especially when you built to a crescendo at the end of the song.

COMICALLY BLOWING OUT THEIR CHESTS, THEY BURST INTO AN IMPROMPTU RENDITION OF

VIOLET and EDIE together

Rose of England breathing England's air,

Flower of liberty beyond compare.

While hand and heart endure to cherish thy prime

Thou shalt blossom to the end of time.

THEY COLLAPSE IN PEALS OF LAUGHTER WAKING UP JACK IN THE NEXT ROOM

JACK STARTS TO RUMMAGE THROUGH TIN
BOX

VIOLET: Aye, I hope we find a good local where we're going.
And a cheaper corner shop than here – I've just got
these barm cakes because I needed them but not my
usual bits; he's hiked up his charges <u>again</u> – making
a killing before we all go! Well, I'd better get off
and stir mi stew on the stove – there's plenty of it,
should I bring some in?

EDIE: No, I'm sorted, ta.... but you can make some for me
when I come next week to tell you all about our new
place. I've got to come back down to pay something
on my Divi Card for the pram I've put away for our
Lorraine at Smith's on Tatton Street."

VIOLET: (FILLING UP, WIPING HER EYES
WITH THE BACK OF HER HAND, SNIFFING
LOUDLY)
I don't suppose I'll get to see you much after that.
I'll miss you.

THEY HUG CLUMSILY. VIOLET RUSHES OUT.
EDIE LOOKS DOWN AT THE FLOOR, ARMS
FOLDED.
A DISTANT WHISTLE BLOWS.

SCENE 4: KITCHEN
EDIE ENTERS

EDIE: Blimey, Dad – you frightened the life out of me!
Where did you get that whistle from?

JACK: It's here in the tin box – it's from when our Albert
used to referee matches on the gym at Salford Lads
Club. Do you think he'll want it back, Edie? This is
his as well - it's a City of Salford Education

Committee Leaving Certificate stating Albert Jones born 30th October 1934 was allowed to leave school on 22nd December 1949 – he went straight to work on Docks.

EDIE: It's a wonder we all did get to go to school and work after being bombed in the War – fancy bringing us back from being evacuated to Ulverston just in time for 1940 Christmas Blitz.

JACK: Well, yer Mam was missing you all... I must admit it was a scare when there were unexploded bombs in the area and everybody from here in Tyler Street and roundabouts were evacuated to the Seamen's Mission on Trafford Road. When allowed back, we all sat here in the kitchen having a much appreciated, and in war time precious, cup of tea. That was the only time I ever saw your Mam laugh and cry at the same time.

EDIE: It was like the War all over again last year what with the power cuts. Our Albert being on strike at the Docks and Violet's Harry on strike at Agecroft Power Station – blimey. I've got some candles, by the way, to take with us, just in case!

JACK: Well it all kicked off round here with lay-offs at Irlam Steelworks so we're heading right into it. Mark my words, the blighters won't be happy until they shut it down, and the Coal Mines, despite what Scargill thinks.

EDIE: I'm off to check on our Lorraine now, Dad, and then onto Regent Road. Put the telly on in a while and we can have a cosy time before an early night – we've got a whole new adventure starting tomorrer.

EDIE REMOVES HER APRON, PUTS ON OUTDOOR COAT, PICKS UP CANVAS SHOPPING BAG AND LEAVES THROUGH THE KITCHEN DOOR.

JACK (SHOUTS): Watch how you go love, these streets have turned into a bombsite what with all the demolition going on.

CHATTING TO HIMSELF HE STANDS
Let's put this box of tricks away then: mi marriage lines; the kids' birth certificates; Christening records at St. Clement's Church; death certificates; and all the other paraphernalia.

SUDDENLY, JACK BENDS, CLUTCHING HIS CHEST, FALLS BACK ON HIS CHAIR, GASPING, STARING AT THE WALL.

JACK (SMILES BROADLY): Well, hello, Nellie – what are you doing here? Come to see us off from the old house? Tell you what, love, take me with you instead.

SHUTS HIS EYES, STILL SMILING.
SILENCE.

SCENE 5: FRONT ROOM
EDIE TURNS THE KEY IN THE LOCK, ENTERS AND CLOSES THE DOOR WITH HER FOOT. SHE CARRIES A FULL SHOPPING BAG AND A TIN BOWL COVERED WITH A WHITE CLOTH. THE ROOM IS DIM

EDIE (MUTTERING) Telly not on and fire burning low.

SHE MOVES INTO THE KITCHEN

SCENE 6: KITCHEN IN DARKNESS
EDIE ENTERS

EDIE: Here we are, Dad – sorry I'm late, I've been gabbing. Let's get this on the table. I'll fetch the vinegar and butter some brown bread. Dad.... Dad...? Surely you've not nodded off again? You've had your naps today."

PLACES THE SHOPPING ON THE TABLE AND SHAKES HER DAD'S SHOULDER GENTLY. HIS HEAD SLUMPS ONTO HIS CHEST.

EDIE: Dad... Dad.... Oh - NO – NO - NO!

SHE SINKS TO HER KNEES, SOBBING AS SHE REALISES HER DAD HAS DIED.

EDIE: Salford born, Salford bred,

Salford wed and now Salford dead.

FADE OUT INTO DARKNESS – TO VERA LYNN SINGING 'ROSE OF ENGLAND'.

Trouble in the Woods

ANNE WINNARD

CHARACTERS: WOODY THE CHOPPER
RED RIDING HOOD
GOLDIELOCKS
HANSEL & GRETEL

*SCENE: WOODY'S NEAT WOODEN HUT, DEEP
IN THE FOREST
RED RING HOOD CRASHES THROUGH THE
DOOR.*

RED   Help! Help! Please let me in!

WOODY   Hold on there. What's the big hurry?

RED   I'm frightened. I'm lost. I want to go home! I want
             my mother.

WOODY   Well you'd better come in and we'll see what we can
             do.
             As you see, I already have visitors. I'm Woody the
             Chopper. I've not had time for introductions yet, but
             when you have all calmed down, perhaps we can
             begin.

GOLDIE   I'm Goldielocks, and I too am lost. I went for a walk
             in the woods, came upon a lovely little cottage,
             eventually fell asleep, I was awakened by three
             large bears. They chased me all the way here. Oh,

they were so angry! I'm named Goldielocks due to my beautiful silky locks and perfect beauty,

RED   I'm called little Red Riding Hood. My grandma made me this gorgeous outfit. Because I am such a pretty girl, the name has become mine. Everybody just loves me so much.

Gretel   I'm Gretel and this is my elder brother Hansel. We got lost in the woods because our wicked stepmother doesn't want us at home. We were frightened of the witch in a house made of sweeties.

WOODY   I am Woody the Chopper. It is my job to look after this forest. I also look after all the silly folk who get into trouble because they don't obey the rules.

GOLDIE   I certainly was not ignoring the rules of the forest. I was taking a walk, saw the cottage and went in.

WOODY   Did any of the bears invite you in?

GOLDIE   Well, no, but there was no one in. I was hungry. There were three bowls of porridge. I tried them all. The smallest one was delicious, just right. I ate it all. Unfortunately I broke the chair. I went upstairs, found the comfiest bed and fell asleep. I was awakened by all these bears, growling and angry, so I ran away and here I am.

WOODY   Wouldn't you be angry if someone came into your home uninvited, ate your food, broke the furniture and fell asleep in your bed? Of course you would!

GOLDIE   Well if you put it like that. Yes I suppose so. I didn't mean any harm. I'm sorry.

WOODY   Ahh OK. You have learned a lesson. I placated the bears with three large jars of honey this time, but don't let it happen again.

Now it's your turn Red Riding Hood. What have you been up to?

RED   At least I did nothing as bad as she did. I didn't break into a house, vandalise it AND steal food. I was guilty of nothing. I was going to see Grannie to take her some food.

WOODY   Did you do as your mother told you? I don't think you did!

RED   OK. So I wandered off the pathway, sat in the shade for a while. I also drank the lemonade mother had made for Grannie. It was so hot and I was thirsty. I ate some of the lemon drizzle cake too. Grannie wouldn't mind.

WOODY   How do you know? You didn't ask her.

RED   I forgot everything because a wolf chased me. He was so fierce. I wanted to get to Grannie's before he did.

WOODY   Fortunately I managed to get there before he did any damage. I can tell you, it wasn't as easy to appease him as the bears! He said any more trouble from you and he will have you!

RED   I won't ever leave the pathway again. I'll do as I am told from now on.

WOODY   And now you two. You've been littering that forest pathway with crumbs and stones – those stones could really hurt someone if they're not careful. But it was really naughty to eat the old lady's house and push her in the oven. Hansel, you're old enough to know better. Can you explain yourself?

HANSEL   We were only trying to leave a trail so we could find our way back home and we were very hungry when we came to the old lady's house.

GRETEL   He's right and it tasted so good.

WOODY   If you had done your school work properly you would have been able to read the signs for the way home. Just like Red Riding Hood here, you must never eat anything unless you're told you may. I got to the old lady just in time to pull her out of the oven. I've repaired the holes in the roof that you ate.

KIDS   We are very, very sorry and will behave in the woods next time.

WOODY   Come on children. Let's get you all home safely. I assume you have all learned by your mistakes and hope you never repeat them. You still have a lot to learn. Let's get going.

Other Publications by SWit'CH

MY LIFE AND OTHER MISADVENTURES

ISBN 978-1-326-60665-7

By Alan Rick

A collection of humorous and poignant nostalgic reminiscences covering Alan's early school years in the war to national service in Egypt.

Alan looks askance at the society of the day with a wry, knowing, smile.

SWITCH ON, WRITE ON, READ ON ...

ISBN 978-1-326-73-48-2

Approx. 200 page showcase of the creativity of local writers based at Critchley Café Swinton.

Containing nearly sixty humorous, whimsical, thought-provoking, ironic, and eclectic writing.

L - #0078 - 121218 - C0 - 210/148/12 - PB - DID2390028